CLASSICAL ILLUSIONS

JASCHA KESSLER

CLASSICAL ILLUSIONS

1985

McPherson & Company

CLASSICAL ILLUSIONS

Library of Congress Cataloging in Publications Data

Kessler, Jascha Frederick, 1929-
    Classical illusions.

    I. Title.
PS3561.E67C55   1985   813'.54   85-8982
ISBN 0-914232-74-6

ACKNOWLEDGMENTS

Some of these stories first appeared in the following journals: *Kayak, Ascent, The New Lugano Review, Gallimaufry, The Kenyon Review, Confrontation, Agni Review, The Spirit That Moves Us, Prism: International, The Smith, The Michigan Quarterly Review, The Missouri Review, Chelsea,* and *The Gramercy Review.* "Hermes" and "Xanthippe" first appeared as the volume *Bearing Gifts,* Treacle Story Series 9, Treacle Press, 1979.

CONTENTS

THE FOUNDATION

THE FEBRUARY RAINS ARE ending here in Southern California. The sky is a flat, light turquoise hue this morning. On the plum and apricot trees in my garden the buds are swollen, their tiny white nipples tipped with a rusty pink. Hummingbirds dart about the orange trees, which are covered with white blossoms clustered among dark green leaves, all washed and polished, free of the dust and grit blown in from the deserts to the north and east during the January heat waves. All the lawns are sparkling with last night's late shower, and the male robins, on their passage north from Mexico, are tugging at the worms that have surfaced or pouncing on the grubs newly hatched, five or six plump brutes together, not at all battling for nesting territory, since their speckle-breasted consorts are still a week behind them in the migration. Spring has arrived.

With springtime too come letters of rejection. The mingled scents of orange blossom and nightblooming jasmine, though rich and syrupy on the cool washed air flowing in from the Pacific, are not enough to lift one's spirit. This year I am not sanguine, for I think my project cannot have interested the foundations, much as it concerns me. Deafened words. My thesis has asserted itself

1

irresistibly over my lifetime. How? Because I have noticed a change. Not in myself, but in those addressed. I have not changed my text: the masterwork is the same. The creation remains vivid—suggestively, eternally new. And yet, scanning the faces before me, watching ballpoint pens suspended above blank notebooks, drawing tangled webs in the vague air, I have begun to perceive the sentence I utter appear to dissipate before reaching their minds. Although they seem to listen hard. *The Words Are Deaf.* I put my thesis: it is language: the world is passing through a cloud of unknowing: the living word is scrambled in its passage between lip and ear: yet the earth endures: here are the robins, the orange blossoms: here morning sun and cool vapors rising from wet roofs.

In the mail there is a letter for me. The large envelope is an impressive, heavy parchment. I open it and remove a single white sheet of the same quality. It has been twice folded. When I have spread it crackling before me on my desk it is elephant folio size, covered with dark words written in clear, bold Uncial hand.

It says, simply: "Welcome! We, Lords of Perigord, and Curators of the Abbey of Thélème, take pleasure in greeting you on your entrance into our community. We are delighted that you have accepted our invitation. We trust your stay will be long, your study original. You will find treasures waiting here for you. May we call your attention to the Caves. Most especially to the caves beneath the Caves. Which caves have Caves hidden within. The rest is up to you. And so forth!"

I turn the letter over. Nothing more is written. I turn the envelope over. Nothing else is written, as if my name and address were enough for the message to reach me. A grant, an odd sort of grant. No funding, no termination. Only a fool would accept.

SPHINX

<hr>

ONE EVENING in July I was walking the dog. It had been a scorching day, and very smoggy. First Stage Alert all afternoon. Now, at eleven it was tolerable, though still hot: the air was smoke-singed and tasted bitter because there had been no rain for seven months—yet another drought year in Southern California. Sirens whooped a few blocks away on the boulevards north and south, fire engines hooted, and the hot night's din roared everywhere. It was, however, relatively quiet down the dark side streets.

From one of the little frame cottages built in the early decades of this century, a faint voice called. I stopped. A cat perhaps? But it had called to me, I thought. In the faint street light filtering through the cedars the house appeared to be a forest green faded with age, the color of stagnant algae staining a swampy pool, streaked with the black tars that drip from our skies. The grass of the lawn was dead in patches and rank with dried mustard weed. The cottage was surrounded by huge clumps of spikey agave cactus. It was a woman's, or child's voice, calling to me for help. The dog crouched, whining. I went in.

The place was cobwebby, layered with stale dust,

filled with a fetid, desiccated air, as though not a window
had been opened in many years. It had the sour taste of
newspapers that have crumbled over a lifetime into micro-
scopic flakes that float about, clogging, gagging the throat.
A house, I thought, like Miss Haversham's, though I wasn't
aware of having had any great expectations. I walked
through the empty, cluttered parlor and stopped. From the
back there came the piteous voice again: an old woman's
quaver. She was crying to me for help. I went down the
fusty hall to her bedroom where I found the poor thing
lying all helpless on the floor. I lifted her in my arms. She
weighed no more than a child. Her skin was scaly, and dry
as a serpent's. Her hair was tangled, sour and clotted, and
she had dry sores on her cheeks. Her dark eyes were
luminous in their shadowed hollows, lit by feverish points,
and her lips were stretched and chapped over her dry,
protruding dentures. A sack of bones she seemed when I
had laid her out on her huge rats' nest of a bed, and she
moaned a little in pain and hunger, her arthritic hands
barely able to hold the glass of water I fetched to her mouth.
Two diamonds were set in her huge old earlobes, sparkling
in the dim glow from a little crimson lamp on her night
table. On her knobbly fingers she wore a ruby ring, a great
star sapphire, and a lustrous pearl the size of a cherry. I
opened the shutters, though she feared the draft, and I let
in what weak, hot air there was outside. She was grateful
then. Her voice was cracked and hoarse, and yet piped like a
child's too. Hardly a voice at all, but a miaowing and a
rasping. "Are you married, young man?" I have gray hair, I
said, and a wife. "Children too?" She gave me those, I said,
and the dog. "Then you are a happy man," she said,
coughing again as she sipped the water. Yes, I answered.
"Well then, remember what I say. What *you* predict comes
true." Of course, I said. She closed her eyes, slitted them

rather, and leaned back against the headboard, her long jaw thrust forward, the waxy teeth protruding even further so that she whistled and clacked. "Don't be too sure!" she said.

I told her I'd call the social services people when I got back home. And I did that.

A few weeks afterward, I saw a realtor's sign on the lawn. In two months, nothing remained: the bulldozer came and razed her house into a mound of splinters in an hour; the trucks came and carted it all away by noon. Three months later there was an apartment building with twenty units and a swimming pool and sauna on the site, fresh new bluegrass on the lawn out front, and the realtors' pennants advertising vacancies. Within two weeks those were gone, and the garage below filled with Jaguars, Stingrays, Cobras and the like. The drought broke: we had November rains washing our city clean again.

A lawyer's letter came in December. She'd left me everything. When the estate was finally settled there would be a quarter of a million. A small fortune for us. A week later, another letter came: her distant relatives were suing: they had been displaced by me: I was an interloper. They claimed that I had dared to trespass; that I had found the old creature dying, and forced her to write me into her Will. That I was a criminal, a fraud. That I was the usurper. And that I would never have dared to enter her bedroom if I'd been a happy man.

Of course I explained to the Probate Court that I was only an innocent. That I had done a mere kindness one late evening, called out of my way. That her own family had left her there on the floor of that midden to rot. That I never expected thanks for doing what is right, let alone the property and a fortune.

The verdict came in the spring: Not Proven.

RHADAMANTHYS

Of ALL TIMES for my car not to start. Late for the last lecture. He'd promised a summary discussion touching on all that he had to teach us, including such problems as had heretofore resisted our reasonable formulation: the source of judgment, the distribution of responsibilities between the logician of the left hemisphere and the esthete of the right hemisphere, and the unplumbed well of energy from which flows love and death in a single yet ambiguous stream labile in nature as time. Etcetera.

I had to roll the car down out of the driveway, after calling the garage for the towtruck. They came along and laid on the jumpcables in ten minutes, after which I drove there to have a hot charge put on the battery. That took half an hour more. Even so, I arrived only fifty minutes late... to find the others shuffling out. At the lectern stood Professor Freud, stacking examination booklets. I murmured an apology for my tardiness. I had not been late before, in fact. He raised his eyebrows at me quizzically as I panted, winded from the three flights I had taken loping. My car wouldn't start, I said. He grunted, sceptical. As far as I was concerned, it was a likely story. I knew better than to insist on the truth. Instead, as was I believe my right, I simply asked him what was going on here.

In that low voice of his, that voice nearly a whisper, and which had caused us to lean forward tensely week after week just to catch his precise utterance, he observed simply that I was too late: "I have just given you your final examination."

But this was to be your last lecture, I protested. The exam's next week! "I am sorry for you," he shrugged. Sorry! How could you have done this! Whom does it serve! Time is needed in order to think! You promised to review all this matter in the end! "Yes, I have usually done so. Nevertheless, I decided to give the test today, and finish things up for good." He indicated with a wave of his hand the questions written in small, Italic script on the blackboard with dark blue and bright yellow chalk. For a moment I studied them, uncomprehending. They seemed to be nonobjective statements about our everyday life; they had nothing to do with the themes he'd discoursed upon all these many weeks. And who could have answered them in this one brief period we had? Fifty minutes for essaying Process & Probability; Work, Waste, & Compensation; Appropriating Silence? And other topics too! I said, But surely, Professor, I can make it up? I'm perfectly willing to take another exam whenever you wish to give it. "No, no," he whispered smiling, "now that you have seen my questions, it is impossible. I will never let you make it up. Too bad. However, I am sorry for you."

I stared at him as he grinned up at me through his crisply-curled salt and pepper beard. He didn't flinch; but he did play for time, fumbling in his jacket pocket for a box of matches, averting his glance as he relit the soggy stump of his short, black Swiss cigar. I said nothing, because I knew there was now nothing to be said.

Still, I stood my ground: he'd have to pass around me to leave the room. Sucking at his cigar, he waited. He knew how to wait. I had to speak at last. So, I said, I've missed my chance. "Yes, well. You came too late, you know." I beg your pardon? I said ironically. He did not reply. Keeping his eyes on me, knowing that I knew that what he taught was now mine in any case, and that he had committed the unforgivable, he gathered up the papers, that firm little man, tucked them beneath his arm, and came towards me.

Naturally I stepped aside. Nodding curtly once, he went out. It was all over. Resisting the rage that gathered in me, a force that seemed to rise from my toes, I drew a deep breath and held it for a few seconds. Then I turned and walked out into the vacant corridor. The Professor was striding towards the exit with that pace he'd learned on his Alpine walking holidays. As he passed through the door he tossed the bundle of examination booklets into a trashbin. Then he was gone, a puff of thick Brasil tobacco smoke hanging in the air behind him. It floated a little while, and thinned away into nothing.

IKAROS

DOWN SECOND AVENUE driving stop and go through racketing thunder and rancid blue fumes in the rush hour, eight lanes of trucks, busses and cars inching towards Manhattan Bridge on the last Friday of June as the sinking sun spreads, flattening, a pale red like an erythrocyte dying. On the corner north of Delancey there's Tuli, Tuli Knoepflmacher. Tall, thin, sloped shoulders. A muzhik's reddish-brown beard to his belt, matted and tangled. Worn Indian moccasins on his long feet, fraying holes in the knees of his baggy jeans, and a black-green tartan flannel shirt draped over his small behind. It must be Tuli. I sit jammed behind a garbage truck halfway up the block. I honk him. He's carrying a fat bundle of leaflets under his left elbow, and passing them out to commuters stalled like me on the Avenue. If I know my Tuli, it's more of the same: anarcho-pacifist literature full of tortuous analysis, denunciation, exhortation, excoriation. Terrorism of the sleepwalker, though gentle in its way, because not yet plugged into organized power. I honk him again. His head turns slowly: it is Tuli—those great brown liquid eyes full of dreaming wonder. He stares, and doesn't see me.

9

Seven years since graduation. In fact, we didn't take that last step officially: we strolled away from Brooklyn College through an April shower. Our credits had accumulated till we were far beyond degree requirements. Somebody had run a check on us at last. So we were expelled, with Highest Honors. "What's wrong with intellectual curiosity?" Tuli asked the President. The answer we got was, "Nothing. But you're occupying minority space." "I am a minority of one, sir," Tuli came back sweetly. "Beat it now—before the Comptroller flays my ass!" And it was curiosity that had kept us hanging around, a couple of Phi Beta Kappa bums—as well as yet another undeclared war that was consuming young men's bodies like bulbs in a Times Square marquee. I took shelter working at my doctorate in biophysical chemistry. And I got something nice done with a five-year grant from the National Science Foundation: heart-cell metabolism, functions of lipids, lipoproteins, lipoids, lipolysis. Leading me to my next project: lipoma processes: the fatty tumor, benign and other. My future lies in California: Sunday morning I fly out, and goodbye to all this. But what's Tuli's thing? From the look of him, he's gone right on with his poetry of poverty, his preaching, his principle.

Principle. What we had. Our true plenty. Perhaps. Tuli ignores my horn. He gets hooted all day. He continues shambling among the cars, coming up the line, thrusting his leaflet into open windows, smiling, saying his word of peace—that soft smile says it's peace. When he reaches my rusty, shuddering, blatting contraption, I lean over, throwing the door open. I know he'll recognize me, and I know he'll show neither surprise nor pleasure. Everything is as it is. Even time signifies nothing for Tuli. "Hello," he says in that same low baritone, and flops in. What a smell! Sour as mildew, a Bowery bum's smell. When did you give up on washing? "I wash myself. These are my clothes this year."

Simple as always. Before we're over the Manhattan Bridge and out to my mother's in Flatbush, I know where he's at. While I'm in the library and lab for seven years, he's adhering to principle: honesty, resistance to social warfare, resistance to social crime, resistance to criminal work, resistance to the darkening of intellect and the occultation of the soul as systematically organized in America, specifically emanating from Manhattan, the rock of evil. Twice-married; twice-deserted and annulled. What woman could sue him, and for what? To put him in jail, because he demonstrates we're all prisoners to begin with? When he alone, pacifico-anarchist, struggles toward freedom? And so he does, taken care of now by one friendly female or another: harmless, humorous, helpless. Fed by whoever finds him in the street or climbs the ancient flights to the seventh floor somewhere below Houston Street, to the Clubroom of his Society for Anarcho-Pacifism, where there's the reliable Gestetner duplicator still, cartons of blank paper, a coffeemaker, some rickety folding chairs with their missing wooden slats in the seats, the barred windows opaque with fifty years' grime, a platform made of old crates, and the oak lectern from some long-lost school auditorium, the NRA fridge with the coil on top and still working, and mouse droppings everywhere in the corners of this abandoned factory loft. He dosses beneath a thin, khaki Army blanket on a decrepit piece of carpeting laid on a workbench, when it's free of leaflets and stapler waiting to collate the Manifesto. Nothing's changed since I first saw it as an anarcho-pacifist of sixteen. Posters, handbills, proclamations: all the light of the future originates there. He is now its source and messenger, the old leaders being gone, swept away into Social Security and after. The ink-smudged sheets with their red and black letterings do not shout slogans—they argue, reasonably and patiently and impossibly, for the Kingdom of Heaven on Earth...

now...if we listen to the dialectic, and if we hear. Really, it's quite simple, simpler than even Moses could have supposed. Of course it is. But easy it isn't. Whoever said easy? Even falling asleep, even death isn't easy. And yet, why not? As Tuli has said always, "Only drop your mental chains, only reach up, reach out, and soar, up, up, and away...." Gravity, Tuli, gravity, I have replied. So far Tuli's up there still, sustained by friends, ex-wives, fond girls, as though he's winging really on his own into the light. Say one thing for him: unlike the other dreamers, Tuli respects science. And math talent? He proved a fundamental theorem in ergodics at eighteen. Perhaps it scared him. Science is mine too, he said, to enjoy or not, as I choose. He chose his own truth. Which he offers yet. Do I see that? he asks. And I say, I do, I do see, as we sit stalled on Manhattan Bridge, gazing out over the old Navy Yard and the Lower Bay towards the Statue of Liberty out there down towards the southwest. I see us together, Tuli, in midflight over the doubts weltering below, hateful monsters with terrible slashing teeth and ravenous gullets hiding scaly-sheathed in the unillumined depths. From which terror, may we be safe. And we shall be safe, I add— if we're prudent. "Prudent? What's prudence got to do with principle?" Laws, Tuli, there are laws. Many laws yet unknown. Ignorance is dangerous. Willful ignorance is sin. "So you've held. You know me, though." I know you, but Tuli, do you know yourself? "I do, I do," he mutters, looking down into the spreading scarlet stain on the turbulent, gray waters. "And I know that what I must have is more than what I know. It's up there," and he points skyward, "where the light comes from."

So we have resumed the conversation at the beginning, after seven years. No great distance covered, it seems. This has nothing to do with radical thought, or plastic bombs in toilet stalls, a burst of submachine fire in the waiting room, hostages lying against the walls, ankles tied with lamp cord. It's that we're right where we have always been—at the beginning, starting out once again, like waking in the morning. If what happens is waking, when the alarm clock jars. Thirty seasons pass; we grow beards; we work at something; varied bodies come within our reach, and go again. Yet we have not launched ourselves. Our wings are folded. We stand looking out over the surrounding sea that must be somehow passed, if we're to begin to think. Construct a raft? when the shore's patrolled day and night, the waters roughened by wind and current in perpetual conflict? Meanwhile I've found my solution. Tuli though has his principle. And his principle and my prudence will never fly together. Pity.

At my mother's we take a light supper of cheese, salad and sardines and smoked fish, buttermilk, olives, and black bread. Tuli soaks in the shower while she washes his rags and dries them. Before our eyes then, the bum's transformed. Young Tuli once more stands here: curly-bearded, red-cheeked, big, brown, glowing eyes, a shine to his curly locks too, and that clear skin, that light olive complexion that is like a fine suede. Handsome: layers of anarcho-pacifist dirt had obscured him. He waits in my striped robe, that comes down to his ankles, while she patches the jeans. He smiles at us, and we smile back. My mother has always had a tender protectiveness for the poor homeless child, as she calls him. Even for these brief hours she's happy to have him back, so that she may work her domestic magic upon him. "Tuli, Tuli," she keens with joy, "don't throw yourself away, my sweet boy, don't go chasing after a vision. You're still nice. Be good to yourself, Tuli. And listen to me: be a man, after all." He answers her plea simply, "I hear you, Momma." But she knows him better than he knows himself. As we go into the night to hunt up some dames I know down in Brighton Beach, she calls after us, "You hear me, Tuli? So why don't you listen!"

The chicks are okay: we see a good show; take a walk on the boardwalk; spend a long hour after midnight in their pad. Like old times. As we're strolling towards the street where I'd parked, we find ourselves going a dark stretch— streetlights all out, smashed by rocks—and so we review the constellations visible at this late hour over the Atlantic. It's something we used to do, parsing the Zodiac on summer night rambles. Suddenly, we both take an awful fall together—into a hole in the sidewalk two feet deep and three across. Fortunately, nothing's broken, we find on checking ourselves over. We sit stunned for a while at the rim of this pit, rubbing our legs and cursing the Borough of Brooklyn, the city and the society that permits such a clear and present danger to its citizens, in which no one cares enough to remedy even such an obvious evil. It is an execration we used to utter in antiphony, in the old times. And nothing has changed: it's only worse.

We look at one another. We sigh, and get up and work in silence to fill this awful mantrap. Handfuls of dirt scrabbled from the vacant lot here; sticks, stones, tin cans and bottles, whatever broken bricks or chunks of concrete we can pick up from the demolition of the burned-out tenement across the alley. We fill it. Then we stomp on it until it's tamped level with the jagged edge of the ruined sidewalk. A sweaty, frantic hour in silence. We're fouled by the effort. Naturally, there's no water anywhere around here.

On the way to Manhattan, Tuli asks me to stop the car on the Brooklyn Bridge, just as we're passing midpoint. He needs air, he says. Wants to walk the rest of the way home himself, across the Bridge, and up Manhattan to his loft on lower Broadway. I will not argue with him. I can't keep him. We always acknowledge the primacy of desire. Principle, he calls it. I call it anarchy. Anyway, I'm tired, and want my bed. The final report's due in tomorrow. Sunday morning I'm flying to the Coast, and my new lab.

I let him out. At the Manhattan end, I swing around, heading back again. As I pass him and see him striding west on the boards that run down the center of the Bridge, I give him the horn again. He seems to wave, a slim shadow in the starlight.

The week has passed swiftly. It's my first time in San Francisco. There are bridges here too, newer spans, immense ones. A letter comes. Tuli's jumped from the Brooklyn Bridge, and landed in Kings County Hospital. Back broken in three places. In deep coma. Maybe he'll live. Maybe not. My mother's matter-of-fact. Probably, she adds, he'll live: if he can be picked up alive out of the East River at four in the morning, then he can be set back on his two feet to start in all over again.

I write back to say that I've been well-received here. They've waited for my coming. My place in the lab's set out for me, and I can begin to work. I have even landed a nice sublet in a new tower: it looks down on the Golden Gate, on the Bay, and out over the Pacific. I've landed safely, and everything is better than I imagined.

AEAEA

THE THREE VIRGINS, they called us at Vassar. I don't know, even now, if we were wise or foolish. But we've each seen something of life: one in New York, one in Chicago, and one in Beverly Hills. We meet up often enough, passing over this wide wilderness, to and from on the career trails, the marriage and separation trails, wandering from sacking and slaughter with our booty, from conquest and humiliations, wedding banquets and sanatoria, fatfarms, dude ranches and communes, islands en route, and adventures.

The Three Virgins are now divorcees again. And I have been trying recuperation at a fortnight's seminar of sensitivity training in the mountains of California over the Pacific. My gyroscope's almost reset yet again: after the last breakup, which left me stripped and drifting, I feel like I've been refitted for another journey. But where to? What god have I offended, I ask myself, that such stormy mischance rules my way? It's a question that has no answer, I think, because I am not, after all, the only one in these straits. Each of us has suffered her trials.

When my plane landed in Chicago I called Cissie. And

she told me Celia flew in today too. We could have another reunion: it's been a year. There was nothing we'd have to say: it had all been said over and over, for ten years now and more. Cissie as much as indicated that when I entered, telling me to get my fancy things on right away: we're off to a party. Celia was almost ready, and then in she walked from the bedroom, pale and shining. I showered and dressed and made up. Then our brandy toast, the same one as ever, "Bon Voyage!"

The buzzer rang, and Cissie said, "My date, our escort and driver. Be nice to him, girls, he's shy—and loaded." She called into the intercom that we were just descending to him. "Made ten million before he was forty. Corn futures and hog bellies. Retired. Went into training. Now he's a rabbi."

The party's in a penthouse on the Drive: forty storeys up, all glass wall. Behind us, Chicago stretches glittering to the west and out of sight over the horizon. Below, Lake Michigan steaming and heaving as the evening lengthens out. Towards midnight it turns utterly black, nearly invisible, because the July sky is hot and full of low stagnant thunderclouds. These affairs are all the same: white fur wall-to-wall, fifth-rate paintings signed by modern masters on all the walls, ditto lithos in frames that cost far more than the prints, heavy plastic constructions with shifting fluorescent colors inside, cubes or spheres or tall oblongs, and glass and chromed steel abstractions that get in the way. Fifty-seven varieties of hors d'oeuvres.

Cissie and her sweet, plump little rabbi are old hands up here in speculators' heaven. They introduce Celia and me quickly to the possibles among the swillers and boasters. Most of them are not from Chicago, it seems, but had stopped off on their wanderings, and found what they wanted. The great grain terminal and hogbutcher has

enough to hold them fast, and make them rich in less time
than it takes to raise a child to the age when it can be
shipped off to college on its own. A loud party.

Celia settled on a black lawyer about six feet and a half
high, and had gotten far along and down to cases with him
by midnight. "He's part man, part The Machine," she
hissed at me on a pass to the john. Sounds okay. He's
handsome, walnutcolored, poised, and looks extra good
among this demotic bunch of crass males, halfbearded,
scragglyhaired, paunchyjowly, pudgypinkies, all snorting
at the trays—but all all-confident and dangerous. These
didn't seem ready yet for the mineral baths and egorevitali-
zation sessions the same types huddle at on the Coast. I
don't know if it's better for them or not: I'd just spent the
last days, as I say, with those identical swingers and
swingees, naked in the hot tubs, touching and stroking and
eyeballing, plumping all the naked misery together in
midlife, under the guidance of the oracular therapist.
Though here they didn't do primal whining and elaborate
charts of their life-patterns. They shouted about politics,
power, campaigns and fixes, and stood before me dressed to
the teeth. But is there a difference, if you look into their
eyes?

Our host is something else again, besides being a
zillionaire, as Cissie prompts me. And with a wife and
grown son. Oh, where? "Iron Mountain," says he, "know
where that is?" Can't even guess. "North, 'way north
of north, top of Michigan. Great country. Mosquitoes,
Hemingway. Got a lodge up there. Fly up weekends, when I
can get away." Right now you're tied up though? "Can't
you see?" and he gestures at the crowd with wide arms.
"They eat me out of my profits. But business never stops
here, you see." I could see. He's forty-five, built like a
rolling barrel; hairy black knuckles over smooth hands

with nails manicured and polished, the little rings with big diamonds bright on both pinkies; shadowed cheeks and cleft black chin, oily skin and bulging, sweaty black eyes; square feet and shoulders thick enough to shove an ox over. And he never stops moving: smoking constantly, eating away at his own rich table all evening, gulping Maalox tablets and washing them down with 20-year-old malt scotch. Booming raspy voice, hoarse from shouting orders into the world. And with it all, a grabber: there wasn't one woman in the place I didn't see him grope in the course of four hours, including me: a paw on the breast, a clutch at a crotch, two hands—between canapes and drinks—on the backside. Wild, inconsequential squeezes. Never a pat or a stroke, no; but bizarre snatches just like those of a nursing child. Only, those hands could hold a good piece of you, and they bruised. It was funny, somehow, and went on in time with his words, his eating, his jokes, his noisy good cheer and domination. It was not funny, either, because it wasn't sex. I have never seen anything like it, in all these years of wise and foolish virginity. Cissie apologized, "I should have warned you. They say he's like that at his own parties. Outside, he has a sense of reality, they say."

I would say that he's a lost man, I remarked. "Yes," Cissie agreed, "and his wife loves him faithfully."

At one a.m. the party broke up in exhaustion. Yet he isn't finished with us. Cissie and her date, Celia and big black lawyer, our host and I are dropping forty storeys in the elevator. Going sailing. His yacht's parked just out there where the green light's blinking at the end of the dock, and it's waiting for us now. ESCAPE II. A big sailboat. Sleeps ten. At the gangway, the rabbi stops, holds up a forefinger, looks about at the heavens, the low dense clouds glowing pink and white from Chicago's grid, and intones, "My children, no wind, and it's coming on to rain. Let us go home to bed on dry land. Today's another day." Cissie stands there frowning over the water in the middle of the plank, lifting her silver lame skirt to her knees, and mutters only, "For crying out loud, Jonah." Our host drives us all aboard, and before we know it, he's got her untied, cast off and moving out. The black lawyer's wearing a fancy yachting cap full of gold braid like a commodore: he's got the galley opened up, drinks coming, and we are slowly shoving along into Lake Michigan. Host has turned into captain, with a sailor blouse tugged over his burly chest, a pair of anchors embroidered in gold thread on the collar, and tucked in crooked behind: his hairy feet are bare on the planking: he's raising canvas with mighty haulings: and then he's running up and down, placing us in our positions, yelling at us and bellowing out nautical phrases at Cissie, Celia and me: "Lee, there! Hardalee! Mizzen mizzen! Belay that tackle, matey!" And somehow, we get far out into the darkness before we know what has happened.

The lawyer is now seated before the mainmast, his yachting cap down over his brows, a tall drink in his lap. Before slumping into sleep, he says, "Always wanted to sail away from that place. Shit."

And all the time this voyage has been getting under-way, our captain has been a demon of action: shouting, swearing at us, sweating, grabbing at hunks of cheese and bread, pouring glasses of scotch, lurching up and down the length of his sailboat, squeezing our tits at every pass, commanding the sleek ESCAPE II as though it's headed for war. But there's no getting out of this now. Where are we going? I ask finally, struggling with the wheel, first left, then right, trying to understand his ejaculations. "Ten points alee! Bring her about, blast you!" and so on.

"Yar, Yar! Keep it yar, girls, that's the only thing that matters now."

Well, it seems our destination is still Chicago, up the Lake Shore somewhere, "to the Northwestern," whatever that is, a new jetty at his new corporate offices maybe. Though there's nothing out there in any direction now: utter darkness. We're exhausted. Not him: he's eating, and burping, and groping at us alternately every time he passes alongside and shows us "how to make yar." And despite it all, the three of us are laughing: our long skirts flung aside, our shoes and stockings stripped off. The three of us in the hot air filling the world over the lake waters, pale white shadows in the gleam of the running lights, wearing only our bras and panties, our hair coming down wet and wild, Cissie wearing her glittering necklace and Celia with her diamond earrings and bracelets . . . and he in his sailor shirt and jockey shorts—some crew.

But we get nowhere at last. Three a.m. Dead, flat calm. The lawyer wakes up and says simply that in the absence of any favorable wind, the best thing for this expedition to nowhere would be swinging round and going back. Our captain's standing behind me, pressing hard up against me, his arms covering mine, his hands clasping my hands to the spokes of the wheel. "How the hell do we do that?" he says. "Well, switch on your diesels, man, and put her about southeast or something."

"The hell you say," he roars, holding me there. "That's not yar. I want everything yar, yar, dammit! and yar it'll be, or nothing!"

And so we wallow into the first weak gray of dawn, which reveals the east to us, and nothing more. A fine, thick mist of warm rain envelopes ESCAPE II. Shivering, halfnaked under a blanket, looking like poor strayed cows, Cissie and Celia huddle curled up in the arms of the black giant against the mast up front. And I stand pinned to the wheel, the compass floating dreamily in a slow circle before my eyes, while our captain paces stubbornly behind me, drinking, munching, lecturing the greasy swell of green-gray waters. Yar, I could tell him, is nothing. And nothing's yar. But I don't.

CHEIRON

NOW LOOK, SIR, excuse me—you mean he takes the poison willingly?" Yes. "Because he thinks he's not coming back?" He knows it. "It's goodbye, just like that?" Yes. "All right, say he can do better than become a shitbeetle or lizard like us. But he could escape from prison, and teach us how. So we could make it to a bear, a baboon, a porpoise even?" That's all over now. He's going on, going out, going up.

Ames throws himself back in his chair, wincing as if he's been clubbed. The others are silent, drowsing as usual or fiddling with their pens or staring up at me, as puzzled as he is. Their eyes are clouded with ignorance. They are young. Ames rests his head against the cinderblock wall behind him. Its rough, ashgray surface makes his straight, thick, darkblond hair look like a muddy patch. His eyes are brown, his face long, the skin a dulled pink with rusty, flaring cheekbones. He knots his brows in pain, his thick lips drawn tight.

Two days ago he was baffled by the Ladder of Love. For fifty minutes he grasped it, rung by rung, ascending carefully, a creature made to climb. And then, near the top,

hearing that there was another step, and learning that it
led to the highest kind, but seeing it looming far beyond his
reach, inexplicably distant, he hung there, biting his lip so
hard it bled. What troubled him? "Yes, I see it, sir. But—"
Well, Ames? "—it has no reason from within itself." The
others were confused, vexed by his protest. They shifted
uneasily in their seats, as if they'd felt a wave of nausea
passing through them. Ames looked down because he'd felt
drops of blood on his hand. Holding it before him with
horror, he'd reached for his handkerchief with the other
and dabbed at his chin. I'd watched that blood trickling
down and said nothing: he'd been listening hard to the
silent argument that filled the air in this room, turning and
unfolding. Finally he'd said, "So, he went to this old
mysterious wisewoman to learn the reason?" Yes. "And
what did she tell him?" She told him what he says she told
him. "But it's a secret!" Yes. "And after that, there's even
more?" Yes. "I don't believe it." Suit yourself. "But he
did?" We know only what is reported here. "What is
reported here ... Sir?" What is it, Ames? "It comes from a
witch!" Whom else? Ames had dropped his head. One hand
held the bloodied handkerchief to his mouth, the other
drummed its fingers on the opened, blank notepad before
him.

This morning he doesn't drum with exasperation. He
writhes in silence. One can only wait. We all wait with him.
Ames will bring it forth, when he finds it. He stares out the
window. February in the Mohawk Valley. The hills and the
valleys have been buried ever since early November
beneath layer upon layer of snowfall, each packing on a foot
over the former crust. The brief thaw of late January had
glazed the world with ice, coating the trees, their limbs,
branches, twigs, with a sheath of crystal: the woods
beyond the nearby golf course are a stiff, glistening

network of diamond cables and wires by day, a glowing scribbled frieze by starlight. The very earth seems to have stood still during the week's cold snap: bright and blinding during the short days when the thermometer crawls up to ten degrees, and blueblack during the long, still nights that crack and glitter at twenty below. The porches are menacing cavemouths, with long fringes of heavy, murky stalactites. When we walk in our thick boots over this blanketed, cold world, the ground crunches dryly. Everyone marvels, feeling good because it's not the usual moist and storming sleet and snow tumbling down from low swarms of brutal dark clouds, but hard, clear, opened outward to the vast space of the illimitable heavens. The sky is white with visible cold again this morning, the dazzling, refracted glare of the small cold sun above. We wait, staring out at the scene. Then, three crows come across the panorama of the wide window. Flapping heavily, slowly, patiently, halfgliding, halfwinging, they pass above the shapeless, smoothly-contoured earth, seeming to float on a swift current upwards toward the crest of the hill. Their cawing pierces the thermopane, a conversation of cynical, braying sarcasms. Easily they swoop up, circling suddenly, slipping over the other side for good.

Ames speaks abruptly, "But it's not fair!" Fair? "What about us?" Who, us? "All the rest left behind here. Grandfathers, husbands, and young people. Mothers, babies. Abandoned forever." So it seems, Ames. "Doomed here. Cockroaches, mice, frogs. Snakes and slimy funguses. Your dog, your cat—they were living souls once." Perhaps, I say. "But he has no right! He can't leave us here like this." Ames' face mottles up, his eyes filling with tears. Some of the others smile at me with happy derision; some turn to stare at him. You have a point, I say: it is unfair...but what can we do? "He just swallows that poison and goes

away, when he knows we have no chance of making it to
the top of his ladder, of getting out of all this down here.
Well, I won't buy it—we have souls too." And you think
each soul is entitled to salvation? "Hell, yes." I mean,
Ames, you'd better wait for Jesus then. He'll come along in
a few centuries to fish you out of the pool of oblivion. You
can sing along with the Christ in heaven, and not freeze
beneath the eternal ice of creation like a beetle waiting for
Spring. "I haven't got three hundred years to wait for
Jesus." Too bad. "So, he just turns his face to the wall,
forgets his friends, and passes on. It's cruel. I need his
answer now." But you have it, Ames. "I do?" Yes: he's
asked you for a favor, Ames. "What's that, sir?" Sacrifice
your rooster to Asklepios for him. "Why should I?" In
payment for having been healed. "Now I don't understand
you either, sir." Folding my arms over my chest, I say:
Death, Ames, is the cure.

Now they burst into laughter, all but Ames. Unsure
laughter: for a moment their ignorance has cleared, and
they rejoice in clarity. Will they remember in an hour,
before their thought is turbid once more? But Ames is
angered. "Not me!" he shouts, "not if I have to come back
like some mangy weasel in some godforsaken hole. And
that's only if—if I'm lucky."

The bell rings. Ames slams his chair back into the
cinderblock wall, scoops his books together. The noise of
his raging is obscured by the crashing, sliding, grinding of
the other chairs in the room, the stomping of heavy boots,
and the fading laughter of the others. He leaves by the rear
before I can shake him from his stubborn dismay with a
kind, lying phrase.

Despite the steel frost, it's a busy weekend beginning
for the College. Parties; the place overrun with girls from
Wells, Vassar, Skidmore, even distant Holyoke. Cars

slithering over the ice, smashing crudely into snowbanks; crowds of young people struggling up the Hill or whirling down again on toboggans from party to party, intoxicated and wild in the bonebreaking chill; the girls' laughter and shrill cries audible from far off through the limpid atmosphere. Hundreds of lively bodies: some even wearing shorts and sneakers, their hardy knees red with cold. We older ones stick to our own bars generally this weekend, after the Friday night cocktails. Too much develops in these mixers for anyone over thirty to take for very long: whole cellars awash with beer so that one must walk through on planks; armchairs with half-undressed, longhaired beauties floating by; deafening bands, mad dancing and dozens of bodies heaving on the floors of the wide fraternity ballrooms in the dark small hours. And yet, after two nights and days of this intense festival, there they are Sunday morning walking in the light between the walls of snow, brightfaced and innocent, to Chapel, where our kind, good Colin—a Shakespearean actor before becoming a pastor—delivers them a savage lesson from Calvin's primer.

Late Sunday evening, I stand before the deep punchbowl, lapping up steaming, spicy, mulled red wine provided by our Assistant Dean, a sociologist. Sidney wishes to become the Dean: he hopes that they will come to think it's time at last for a social scientist to take over from the tradition-bound classicist drunk. Being men of business, the Trustees should have sense, he thinks. But of course they are alumni of this place too, and loyal to the dimmed past. In the middle of my conversation with chaplain Colin on the limits of unmediated pain, and the blessings of our needful anodynes of which the greatest is oblivion, Sidney interrupts to ask me what I think of young Ames. I look down at this short, plump hypocrite and reply, An intense boy. "Well, he's gone," Sidney says. His work is okay, no reason for him to drop out in midyear. "He's gone, I said. They took him off an hour ago. Maybe he'll live." Sidney rolls his bulbous eyes upward, a sort of chipmunk he seems to me, puffing his cheeks out with easy words. I dip my cup into his bowl again and ask what has happened.

"We don't know. I thought you might," he leers, prompting me. I answer by raising my cup overhead, pouring a bit over the tablecloth, and drinking it down in one gulp. "The fellows say he got liquored up Friday night early at the start of the Chi Rho mixer. He was in and out of things. They had a big one over there, looking their prospective pledges over. The usual. One fine lassie from Wells says he took her on a talking jag, and she missed most of the dance. Then he went silent, she says, and disappeared."

Which tells us nothing, Sidney. What happened? "He disappeared. At four a.m. they found his clothes outside the gym. Twenty-five below by then." So? "So he was gone. They say he flashed in at the Alpha Delts', the Tau Omegas', and who knows where else. Drunk out of his mind, or whatever. And naked. In that frost. With a wreath of withered oakleaves for a scarf. With a hockeystick in one hand, and a dead, plucked chicken in the other, for Christ's sake! They couldn't catch him. He ran through the Houses like a demon, screaming and getting everybody up." What was he saying? "Nobody knows. Made-up words. I thought you might know."

I dip my cup again, and look down at Sidney. I know how to wait. Sidney coughs. "They found him in the woods out back on the other side of the hill over the golf course. Stiff and blue. Covered with crusted, icy blood. Must have thrashed through the woods. Maybe they'll pull him through. He won't come back here."

Did you call his people? "You don't think much of me

as a Dean, do you." Your wine, Sidney, is balm to me, I say. "Of course I called them. Ames did too sometime during this weekend. Told them some nonsense about breaking out. They thought he had one of his allergic spasms, and advised him to lay off sweets for a while. They're Christian Scientists, you know." Are they really, I say. "He also told them he wouldn't let himself be caught by the Greeks. They suggested he avoid the frat-rushing and go Independent if he liked. Maybe that's why he tore through the Houses, you think?"

Sidney, I can't say. "Well, I thought you'd be the one to know." Why? "Because in the ambulance he came to for a minute, and seemed to think you were there. His mentor, sort of?"

I guess he won't make it here, is all I say. "Perhaps that's what bothered him? Every year some don't," Sidney opines, ladling me out another cup of the hot wine punch, "and it's hard to tell which ones will, and which ones won't. I believed Ames was one of the strong ones."

So he was, I say. "I never believed he would be exceptional, though." Lots more where he came from, I say, hordes of them out there.

Sidney lights another cigarette, looking up at me accusingly. "You are an inhuman bastard." His folks must be very rich, Sidney, for you to be so upset about it. "Very, very rich."

With that bitterly spoken phrase, Sidney dips up a cup of wine, not for me, but for the President's wife, who has been expecting him to come and serve her. I dip for myself, turning back to the chaplain, who observes, "God only knows why there has to be so much pain in this affair."

And He's not telling, I say.

HERMES

CASUAL AS ALWAYS, careful too, I sip my Lillet at the little white cast-iron table in the garden near the freely-turning mill wheel. The mill turns, the water splashes, grinding only the hours away. The willow's very old; its cooling ombre reaches far out over the thick, viridian turf that plunges, dank, moss-lumped, over the bank of the brook purling out from under the ancient building whose dark granite blocks are blackening with lichen. Two silver swans float in the pool behind the weir, and a waddle of young geese gossip as they strip away at the waterweeds near the opposite bank. But for the telephone wires going out over there, you would hope you were in the slower times of the last century, when such afternoons might have been enjoyed for their own sake. An occasional fatty and spiced cloudlet wafts invisibly past from the kitchen: this house is now a country inn on the southern reach of the Cote d'Or. Three Star. Those who know pause here before tooling up to Beaune for the auctions after the grapes are put away. I come a week early, park the aging Aston-Martin conspicuously out of the way—all waxy silver and chromed wirewheels—and wait. I am neither alive nor dead. I just happen to be here. It's but one of the possible seasons of the year on my regular Continental Tour. I'm not expected here, as I might be in Cannes, say. Cannes isn't for me, not even the film fair. Once too often was once too much. Well, one adapts to circumstances. Anyway, I prefer these old heaps of stone along the roads. Why not work from them, if one must? So I break from the gate in Burgundy, Station One. I have various private names for the twenty fortnights of my working season. This one is named after the house: Le Moulin d'Argent. It has been lucky for me.

An ancient district. As you walk into town from the inn, you pass beneath a Roman arch, a great gray square pile over the road. Up a steepish street to the dusty Place de la Liberte, a gravelled square bordered by tall chestnut trees. This month it's filled again with that broken-down gypsy charivari. After my aperitif, I stroll round, always stopping to pot a few clay pipes on the turning wheel with the old toy rifle at a dear 5fr. per load. By now I'm acquainted with the tricks of this crazy gun: I break a dozen pipes each time. Grandpa's patient with me, for a Frenchman. Of course, I let him keep the change from a 50fr. note. Money still buys tolerance. Not everywhere; but in these less-visited spots, yes. And I hand over the stuffed animal to a little girl from the orphanage. A week, and I've given eight of the silly critters away. The Sister takes care to send a different child wandering out of the file towards me after I've done shooting. They watch solemnly, complicit: there is breathless silence until monsieur puts the rifle down, receives his prize, and turns at the applause, delighted to see the children halted on their promenade, as though they happened along just as he was shooting. One reaches such understandings in France. Everything has been known. I can even recall who I am myself, from the soft twitter of the stooped old Sister: "Voila le jeune Monsieur!" That "jeune monsieur's" the sweetest jewel I've ever been given. And I must be fifty by now. Though who's counting.

On my return, there is a fire-engine red Bentley sedan docked alongside my car. Export plates. Only Americans would have one done up in that color: for a gag. Vermilion leather too. I think my party must be waiting, though I've expected them for a week now. Stroll down the old wagon lane back to the garden for another vermouth. There they are, ensconced at my table in the deepening double shade of dusk, their faces blanked by huge sunglasses with mirror lenses. Their heads turn to follow me. What can they see? I hesitate, and they gesture: will I join them? They have surely appreciated the taste of my car, the sort of vintage machine their sort rally in at Palm Springs. Nice folks, the Greens, Hank and Marge: accommodating. Tuxedo Park, New York. Floating awash in their own gravy. Thrilled at finding this inn, nearly empty too, after having been lost a whole day coming from Lausanne over the wild hills and getting miserably stuck in a rainstorm somewhere back there in those forests, not a bed to be found, my God! Switzerland bordered by Appalachia . . . but is this house as good as the Red Guide indicates? Better, I say. Terrine is unmatchable for 50 kilometers. Crayfish hors d'oeuvres should not be missed. Take the whole menu gastro-nomique, I suggest, just as it's offered, day by day: at 75fr., and with old Chambertins, they can complete each day in sheer delight, and so cheaply too. There are also a few things worth looking at in this place.

"We didn't plan to stay," says Marge.

"There's a schedule drawn for us," says Hank.

"Golly, though it's quiet here. What's to see, any-how?" says Marge, opening it for me.

The Last Judgment over the portal of the Cathedral, for one thing. That's worth an afternoon.

"For that nonsense?" she snorts.

It's fine stonecarving. You'll look at it, and you'll see. And that Eve swimming naked on her side like a mermaid, offering her fruit to the man she loves—who wouldn't taste of it?

"Well, all right. Maybe."

"It's not that strict, honey," says Hank, lighting up a three-dollar Monte Cristo, and ordering another double scotch-and-soda. He commences telling me that they're actually headed to some big affair next week, by invitation. Oh? Well, it seems his senior partner at Bache, Halsey and Stuart's an Honorary Chevalier de l'Ordre du Tastevin... something from his mother's side, Hank thinks, vineyards they picked up under Napoleon...and quite the gourmandizer Charley is! but the poor fellow's suddenly off to China next week—you go when they call you—some oilwell-drilling deal...Bee, Aitch and Ess means investment banking, in case I didn't know... Well, of course I do, I say: I've worked with your folks. "You have? What line?" I'm in the communications thing, I reply, groping. But Hank knows all about that: not that he's done any of the underwriting for the new satellites over the Pacific; but he knows—and what is my part? I satisfy him with: a piece of the pickup-relay mechanism, a couple of patents on some resonators: an idea I got from my training in music. That nonsense was enough for him, after I'd told him the Aston-Martin was my first purchase with the first royalties. Hank likes my wheels, Marge approves the cut of my Beverly Hills tweed jacket, the discreet suede walking shoes... So, they're carded to the Tastevin shindig? Then this little inn can start their training, is my suggestion. You don't want to seize up with indigestion: you'd better build to it. "That so?" says Hank, disbelieving. Sixty courses of Burgundian cuisine in three days—just about the richest on earth these days. "My goodness," Marge exclaims, "I'm going to have to run the dogs myself when I get back." Dogs?

And Marge gives me the salient item, as though I were starting to collect an obituary file on her, "I breed Afghans in Tuxedo." Well, I mightn't have guessed that. Golf maybe, from the rangy limbs, the tanned, leathery face, the brown-gold, graying hair cropped straight. But it's dogs. The rings on her hands are interesting: if she travels about in that car, wearing that dazzle of diamonds by daylight, then what's snoozing in the safe back home? Not that I've glanced at them since they'd flashed out as I came into the garden. I go on with my advice, telling them about the Tastevin ceremonies, the chefs' new line of cooking this year, the rare wines they will taste. In response, they ask me to dine, not supposing I would refuse them. Somehow, I'm a little off my feed this evening, I say. "You look spunky enough to me," says Hank, in the way a man tiring of appeasing his lady would. But my way is to send signals on several frequencies, part noise, part sheer redundancy. They pick me up, but they cannot tune in. Making for confusion at the subliminal. Fatigue; then more havoc. I can work faster when they're unaware they can't even discriminate what it is. "What's the matter?" Marge implores, impulsively leaning forward to lay her jewelled paw on my upper left arm, her eyes behind their bright mirrors swimming closer. She presses my triceps, letting her long, freckled breasts droop freely, exhaling a gust of her musk. Though the muscle satisfies her, still I must respond to her concern.

I do, reluctant. My mother's gravely ill, I say. It's upset me. And I'm annoyed too. "Ah," she sighs in that brazen, cracked voice of the first-generation outdoorsy woman. A voice that pleases me, though: it's full of the fret of hard whelping, tennis and lawn parties. Reality that cash buys. She was doing well enough in Bath, I continue, comfortable, considering her age. But she had a whim to see Greece once again—her people came from there, she always said ... "I knew there was something about you!" ... But I think she imagines it: most likely some Classics teacher she once had a crush on—there were such people once in the public schools, you know. "How cynical you are—and your own mother dying!" How did you know that? I say, surprised. "She's sensitive," Hank comes in, suggestively again, patting her knee. "She's a good eye: conformation tells her a lot." Wanhope's wan hope. He would help me to help myself.

I haven't heard from her for ten days. She swore she'd call me here after she got up into her Arcadian hills. "How fascinating," Marge croons, apropos of what? It's down in the Peloponnesus. You wouldn't like it there, it's nothing but dying villages. Never was much more, except for boasting and producing mercenaries. Superstitious from the very beginning, and between Byzantine and Turk, things only got worse. She goes to her mountain, Cyllene. Her father, she calls it, her strength! All nonsense. Pointless. I'm boring you.

"No, no. Go on," Hank says. I don't go on. Why make up more than I must. The past doesn't exist, and there's too much to remember, once you begin to discover it. Marge is titillated and wants more. She is a handy, practical dame, a type easily disoriented by a mystery withheld. She takes it to be sexual. Her nostrils flare. As though sex were still the mystery. Or my dying mother. Fantasy, fantasy. To get hold of herself as we're climbing to our rooms to prepare for dinner, she asks about the ring on my little finger, an emerald-cut yellow diamond of say 35 carats. "That's a real heirloom, isn't it." No, just my father's—he said he'd won it in a poker game on the Orient Express, from one of Goering's boys. "Luck, or skill?" jibes Hank. Both, and more—he had to take the finger with it. That's a deft touch: Marge blanches. When her color comes back, the horror will glow with lust. "I've got things worth a lot more," she says, "but nothing with any background to it." Famished she is, like all these new folks, for history. Which is easily supplied. Harder providing truth. For a reasonable facsimile of that, I go down right away, call Paris and have the telegram sent to me. It will do.

The garçon brings it discreetly two hours later with the check, which I take over protest. We have had a repast of duck and venison and Scottish salmon—I take care to touch almost nothing of the dishes we were sharing about for variety's sake. We have coffee, and light up two more of Hank's Habanas. I am listening to her stories about her shaggy dog. Champion Rondina Tiger Rosay, a silver-and-gold Afghan hound, who took his 69th Best of Breed in Richmond last week. She extracts some polaroid glossies from her Gucci rucksack. Quite a dog, my eyebrows say with amazement. "You must imagine it takes endless hours to get that perfectly splendrous coat." Yes, of course. "Well, no. You couldn't be more mistaken. Grooming him's much less work than that! I never touch Rosie with a brush during the week. He's bathed every five or six days. I use a hair-conditioner by Helena Rubinstein, and I experiment with women's shampoos. Every hair's brushed dry with a 1200-watt blower, and the whole process takes only two and a half hours. I rely on long pin brushes. The longest parts of Rosie's coat are ten inches, and will continue to grow just like human hair. The texture's a pure, beautiful silk, so it doesn't mat. Exercise is terribly important for his coat, since it stimulates circulation."

She must be playing me the tape she uses from one dogshow reporter to the next. I lap it up. She believes she has me now. It doesn't faze Hank. "I roadwork Rosie religiously every day for three miles: he runs beside the estate wagon around the lake in Tuxedo Park, and the last half-mile's straight up the mountain. And proper diet's essential, including balanced vitamin supplements. I'm sort of a health freak," she laughs, "raw meat, cottage cheese, raw vegetables, fruit and about one-third a daily portion of good quality, dry kibble. That keeps Rosie in the pink." I lope ahead to the conclusion: For all those Blue Ribbons? "You got it! I just turned in my 1973 wagon with 175 thousand miles on it. Why, the new one's clocked eight thousand, and that's only over the last two months! I got my first Best in Show with Rosie's mother, a beautiful bitch named Bluejay's Gold Passion. That was in 1973, when Hank was made First Vice-President of Bee, Aitch and Ess. Good year for us," she giggles. "I give Hank a Blue Ribbon, and he gives me a diamond choker to go with the bracelet." Fair enough, I murmur. "Oh, better than that," Hank says, ambiguously. "We both worked our butts off for ten years though, didn't we, darling," she says. "I guess we did," Hank says, and sighs. He will agree to anything. "Of course, it was Hank who revived the Tuxedo Park Kennel Club. That old crowd let it go to hell years ago: too busy in Palm Beach. Someone has to keep tradition up. So why not us?" Why not indeed. Diamonds and dogs. Life goes on. "Hank's busy: busy busy busy. He's a judge of several breeds, and secretary of the Larchmont show too. Oh, not Afghans, if that's what you're thinking! That would be, uh, conflict of interest. After Watergate, it's—" She's at a loss. Hank helps out, "It's not done." "That's what I mean, it's just not done."

But I reassure them, I wasn't thinking that at all. Marge is skeptical. Narrow-eyed, she says, "Then what

were you thinking? Come on, 'fess." I take the telegram
from my breast pocket, hand it over. MAIA DEAD STOP
FUNERAL STOP CAN YOU COME STOP WAITING FOR
YOU STOP LOVE. A tiny gasp of contrition, and sympathy
too. Marge reaches out to clasp my hand in hers. She's
sorry, her eyes liquid. "You must go. We'll miss you, of
course." Hank is very helpful, "Look, don't worry about the
car. We'll putter around a few days. You just go along.
We'll keep an eye on it." I'll garage it, I say, you have
somewhere to get to. "Oh, no!" they protest. Better yet,
since your Bentley's a bit big, why not use my car, and tool
around the back roads: there's lots to see. That's it. They
take my keys greedily. I've tied them down here.

    I go up and get the shoulder bag that's already packed
and waiting. Come down, tell them goodnight, and call a
chauffeur in from town. Before dawn I'm in Dijon. Hop to
Paris. Air France to New York, a first-class nap in First
Class. My kit's in the vault at Irving Trust. Cab over to
Tuxedo Park. Not quite midnight. Rondina Kennels in the
directory. Afghan hounds are silent; the help's asleep.
Sometimes dogs are allergic to strangers, so I quietly drop
by to say hello. The fence is unlocked. Rosie's a friendly
brute, and all his show-training has accustomed him to
visitors. Still, he's restless, alert and smart. A few pats, a
tussle, and then a generous squirt of Mace: he will sleep out
the night. Their house is a big pile of fieldstone: brokerage
Victorian, pre-Depression model. Alarm's an old one too.
Three minutes and I'm inside. Library safe needs thirty
seconds. Not enough in it. There must be more, I can sense
it. Nothing in the master bedroom. The upstairs parlor,
however, is now a trophy room. The new Mosler's tucked
behind an oil portrait of Rosie's mother, Champion Gold
Passion. Blue Ribbons cover the whole wall, and there are
shelves of silver cups and statues of Afghans on pedestals.

Ninety seconds for this one. A nice lot of things, as Marge says, but nothing heirloom. About 250 thou, I guess.

By two-thirty, I'm back in town, closing the bar at the Pierre with a glass of port. And then to bed. In the morning, business: the kit returns to the vault, the glass goes into my Fagin's box on 46th Street. Shlomo's a genuine phony. If you passed a huddle of Hasidim on Sixth Avenue, you wouldn't pick him as the ringer if your life depended on it. Even fasts on Yom Kippur. My estimate's good: quarter-million retail. Shlomo counts me out fifty grand. I might do better elsewhere. But I've known him all my life, it seems. If he ever thought of twisting me, he knows he wouldn't get my ring, an heirloom from Goering's buddy he covets. As long as I wear it, I'm safe from the like of him.

By nine, I'm taking a cognac over the Atlantic. Back on the road to Moulin d'Argent by afternoon. I hope Hank and Marge have enjoyed their two days of sightseeing. As the driver pulls into the court I remember to pin the little black silk ribbon to my lapel. The Aston-Martin's standing there covered with white dust. Good. As I step round to the garden, where they'll be seated under my willow, drinks in hand, I notice on my left sleeve a long and bright strand of silky hair, silver-and-goldtipped, from champion Rondina Tiger Rosay's breast. Nice dog. Nice folks. They'll have a hell of a time at the Tastevin banqueting this weekend. Let them eat till they drop.

DAFNE

INDIAN SUMMER. The Mohawk Valley. The rolling coun-
tryside of Oneida County. On College Hill, actually, out
back on the north side, beyond the football field, following
the fairway as it slopes up and delivers you onto the mount
of the 7th Green, atop which, after putting, you can pause
to survey three small valleys...and consider the conclusion to summer's works. A pattern of greens: cornfields,
beanfields, fields of broccoli, Brussels sprouts, potatoes,
hayfields and stony cowpastures; clumps of maple, oak,
ash and beech copses glimmering aureate, blistering into
scarlet, slowly burning and dropping their shrivelled,
cooling embers to reveal, from this height, their inter-
woven branches that will look like great gray nests for
crows and winter snow. Among them the farmhouses
stand out more clearly now, the roadside hamlets like Paris
and Oriskany and Hinman corners down below where the
creeks wind, those withering old New York wooden houses,
shapeless and shambling, leaning together in peeling
poverty for a hundred years now. Smokes curling in the
still air of October, partly from fireplaces and leafpiles,
partly from the garbage dumps or car bodies forever

smoldering in wreckers' pits that mark these nearly nameless places littered and dying around this harsh region. Here and there the new ranch home or redone Greek Revival specimens of gentlemen farmers, the squires and merchants and bank presidents who prefer the country-side, bleak as it is, to the decrepit cities and industrial suburbs of the long valley to the west towards the Great Lakes far away. A fine prospect though during Indian Summer. Best time of the year. For spring is melting snowpack and running red clay. Summer humid, oppressive, empty. Winter a silent frozen hell of ice glare or howling blizzard of sleet and unending drifting snow-squalls. But in autumn there is that distant view of grayblack foothills to the north, the Adirondacks; and over them, high up, the faint feathered clouds darting through the stratosphere, presaging those ponderous black bellying low clouds that sweep along the ridges and drop the damp, immolating snows of late November. Yet, these few weeks of clarity we have, and vision comes as revelation, as fulfillment before the end.

I am not, this late afternoon hour, mounting the tumulus of the 7th Green, putter in hand, but helping my friend's wife up. We have strolled out here for our last portion of the still and limpid air. It's the Saturday of the annual Sigma Chi Halloween Party. The cars have all pulled away from the football field, crowds scurried off to their various celebrations and cocktail hours. After several years of this regular Halloween bash, we have grown weary of the Sigs of Sigma Chi and their sluttish Vassar dates back there before the First Tee of the golf course. In the hall we have just left, the Sigs, suavely cheery in their Brooks tuxes, snotty and condescending, pouring out bourbon and champagne to the faculty by the insulting case, are introducing their dates, vivid twenty-year-old girls, healthy, fresh-skinned, tireless, stunning in their Bendel and Saks dresses, and flushed with roaring the afternoon away in the football stands, with booze, and brimming over with eager sex. The Sigs and their dates enjoy hosting their professors; they get a sardonic sort of kick from watching their intoxicated teachers weave off into the night, staggering among the fraternity's Porche, Triumph, MG and Mercedes roadsters that lie parked carelessly outside like a few dozen hunters tethered at a country inn toward the close of the great Fall Hunt.

Margaret and I had left them while it was not yet dusk though, to watch the twilight come on, as well as to escape the swelling din of orgy. Her husband was standing with his nose in the 90-proof punch cup, paying court to Prexy, an unctuous ex-minister who'd been brought in by the Trustees to beef up the venerable institution by augmenting sociology, political science and psychology—the wave of the future, as he calls these subjects. He may well be correct: we are working hard at transforming Sigs into lawyers and admen, into our social managers, our chiefs. Canny, these ex-Presbyterian ministers, who are caring properly for this world of ours. Margaret's husband was listening hard to the President, who had remained as usual next to the big bowl to dip his cup frequently and get the obedient attentions of his faculty as they came up and returned for more of the same. Margaret's husband was laughing at all his jokes: he hasn't finished his thesis yet, and his position is still unsure. He is only halfway through a study of voting behavior in the former colonies of Africa, a Harvard idealist who'd helped in formulating their constitutions as a prize undergraduate interning in Washington over the summers. Over the last six years, six of his seven countries have been restructured into native tyrannies, and he is persona non grata in them all; if the records he needs are not destroyed, they are in any case sealed to him. Between that, and Margaret's six-years' barrenness, he has work ahead yet for his laurels. Still, his old preppy ties at Rockefeller and Ford keep him in firewood, and Margaret in gowns like this ivory, gold-embroidery-edged raw silk thing she has on tonight, her fine breasts floating free in it as she takes my hand to clamber up onto the 7th Green. Her shoulders are protected by a thick ermine jacket from the cooling air. For three years now we have been friends. Margaret is happy here after nervous, smug, perverted Cambridge. Her childhood as a poor white in the tobacco-sharecropping hinterland of North Carolina haunts her, but these clothes, the great old college house, and the position comfort her. Great wide eyes and a fine head she carries erect above those sloping, firm shoulders: these ought to more than suffice for her here in this small, closed community among the old Indian hills, populated by pigeontoed and gaunt professors' women or chapped-handed and haggard, pregnant instructors' wives. Often she seems melancholy to me after a few bourbon and waters, wistful. This vestige of her miserable childhood is charming: she had grown up, not as a weed with tiny flowers in some briar patch, but into a handsome, big, velvety magnolia blossom. She walked with a long sway, but proudly tall, and in that white gown, pacing across the 7th Green, her gait was a caryatid's.

"Did you know," she says, "the fruit of the magnolia flower's a spiky, hard, dry, heavy cone, about as big as your fist? We used to throw them like grenades when we were little kids. I have a scar from one too." And she lifts the mass of auburn hair that shaded her cheek: on her left temple there is a faint round set of tiny, stippled scars, like an old smallpox badge. I touched it gently.

Around the valleys strung out below us to the north, to

the east, and the south there are bonfires lighting: they look like torches lifted here and there on those slopes facing us. Too far off for us to make out the knots of children running or dancing about them like savages. The sun has just vanished behind our backs in the southwest, beyond the distant Alleghenies. Oriskany Valley, laid out beneath, is a clear gold, red, black picture puzzle. There are stone markers standing in the woods that show the border of the English colony a little more than two hundred years ago. We are standing a few miles outside that pale, in Indian Territory, up here on the golf course. Margaret has laughed at everything I've said during the last hour. Margaret has smiled at me with affection, tenderly, even when I've said nothing at all. Margaret tonight is gay, yet grave. A handsome woman, but in this twilight now, as I touch that scarred temple, her loveliness stuns me. I see beauty itself. And I tell her so. She smiles, and in that murmuring drawl replies, "Why how poetical the liquor's made you tonight." No, no, I say, it's something about you. "My new gown, child. Isn't it ravishing?"

Look at that! I say. It's perfect: the full moon has come floating up in the east. A primitive artist has painted it a deep red-orange, pumpkin color, laid on for Halloween. The long hill over which it sails gives it rondure. What a pity it would have been to have missed this sight by standing back there in that Sig pen swilling hard punch. But, glancing at Margaret, I realize that she gazes up at it with no joy. Tears fill her wide, green eyes; her hands lie crossed, palms cupping her breasts. Margaret, I say, are you grieving?

The bloody moon's light lies pooled in those eyes as she looks at it. We stand alone in the circle of close-cropped green grass at the 7th Hole, its green now a black platform in the scarlet moonlight. From the gray, old stone mansion of the Sig House—a patch of lights beyond the golf course, behind the pines—comes only the syncopated thudding of the rock band's bass. Margaret tries to answer me. Her lips quiver, but she can say nothing. The tip of her tongue emerges to taste the tear that has trickled down beside her nose, and over her upper lip. I think, I should like to taste Margaret's tears myself. I say, Margaret, what's the matter? A reply, faint, "It's nothing, dear, nothing at all." At a loss, I try, It's beautiful, isn't it. "Yes. For the moment only." Is that what makes you sad? "I'm not sad, really. It's these headaches I've been having. I'm on tranquilizers, you know." I did not. "And they make me laugh, they make me weep. As if I had feelings."

Her words perturb me. "But," she adds, "I don't have them, you know. Isn't that awful?" With a catch of laughter or of tears, a sob, she tosses her head proudly. She is gorgeous. I turn and take her in my arms, consoling. It is awful.

She clings, burying her wet cheek in my throat. For a moment. I don't know what I hold in my arms: the ermine jacket has a thick animal musk, and her breasts against mine shake as her breath comes in broken gasps. A long moment it is, until I feel her calming. It must be some fine animal I have caught in my arms, and now it rests here, without terror. But it's unpredictable, I know. "Oh, look!" she cries out. I release her and turn. She points at the sky near the moon, suffused now with an expanding aura of shimmering golden light. "What's that!" Above the globe of that moon, and far beyond it in space it seems, there's a point of bright light, brilliant as the evening star. It is rising fast, towards the zenith. It is not Venus, for that one sparkles over the horizon at our backs, above the abyss into which the sun has fallen. This wanderer swims steadily, wavering slightly in the tremulous atmosphere. "What ever is that?" she cries again, "it frightens me." Ah, that must be a satellite, I say, one of our space stations. It's picking up the rays of the hidden sun. Look how fast it flies out there.

"Suppose it's one of theirs," she says. "Suppose it's coming for us. Suppose it's carrying the Doomsday Bomb." Ah no, Margaret, I say, stroking her arm, don't even think of it. "Suppose it is, and suppose the end of the world will come in twenty minutes. What would you do!" Her hair is disarrayed, drooping in an auburn-black shield over her cheeks. Her eyes are fixed on me. She has seized my hands in hers, and is pressing them convulsively, as though trying to utter a phrase in sign language. "What would you do if you'd only twenty minutes left to live?" Well, I say, I think I would.... "What!" She's smiling at me, curious. Well, I'd fuck.

Margaret flings my hands away, in disappointment, or despair. She turns away sighing. "Oh, you!" Well I would, I say, coming up beside her where she stands poised at the edge of the Green. Deeply, ruefully, she sighs again. She's staring like a diver down into the wild ground below, the coarse weed stalks of summer gone, down along the disused, rutted path wandering off precipitously to the woods that border the golf course here, a path tangled with fallen branches, deep drifts of leaves clotted with mold and mud. Quite calmly she remarks, "I'm afraid it wouldn't do me much good. My legs are like logs for the first ten minutes, like dead wood. It's all I can do to hold them open, you know. And it takes me thirty minutes to come ... if I do come. Isn't that awful? The world would be over by then. I'm sorry, darling." And she begins to laugh, too loudly now, pointing up at the satellite that has climbed into the velvety black zenith overhead. "Twenty minutes to go," she cries, "only twenty minutes!" I am looking up at that moving point, puzzled.

A violent tug at my throat snaps my neck painfully. She has ripped open the knot of my bowtie. And she's flitting down the steep slope off the Green on her heeled white sandals, dashing along that dark path, running towards the wood, a white, weaving form. I hesitate up there on the high mound of the 7th Green. I hear her clattering through that dangerous darkness down the hillside. I listen to her steps fading. Then her voice comes back, a poignant cry of pain. Then, silence. She must have fallen down there in that obscurity. Like a wounded creature, she is lying in her fine white silk and fur, waiting for an end to it.

TEIRESIAS

SATURDAY MORNING we decided to travel all the way downtown for a change. It was one of those memorable days when March has just blown itself out and April has not yet warmed and gathered its damp tinctures of sulfuric smuts. We were after nothing really but a view of the fast-flowing waters of the Bay, of the Statue of Liberty, and the great bridges arching east and west, and the shapeless forest of gray hulls and masts in Brooklyn, like the dead trees of a great swamp. No one is crowded then in the shadowed canyons of the financial district; on Saturday morning the overreaching walls of stones and glass refract clouds and the sky in harsh cubistic angles. Only strollers, shoppers for oddments, traverse the narrow streets, thinking of hardware, exotic lumber, surplus paper, sundries, electronic gear and salvage. The offices are silent, dark, rank upon rank above the old winding abyssal streets. Alpha to Omega: the first Dutch cowpaths and village tracks, now paved over yet persistent beneath asphalt, enduring the unimaginable mortgaged future entailed in the skyscrapers. Only a very deep, frozen granite plug into the magma beneath the mantle of Terra could sustain the weight piled up on Manhattan Island down there near the Battery. One feels lighter, smaller than an ant in that district. But on such a Saturday morning, noontime, springtime, one's soul caroms about those breezy canyons, free for an hour from the corridors of work in our pharaonic temples.

Up Nassau we wandered after circling the tip from Wall and out along the railing over the sparkling, tangy bay waters. We looked into old stores, with their high ceilings and carved oaken lintels. Now and then, to the east and the north, a glimpse of the high decks of the Brooklyn Bridge swaying quaint and stolid over the East River. We stopped somewhere at the end of Nassau Street before a dusty store window. Judging from the anchors crossed over the first storey, the building must have been a chandler's warehouse in the 1800's. Most of it seemed derelict now, boarded up. But the door was open. Let's go in, I said.

Such an array of ill-sorted junk: hardware, war-surplus equipment and clothing, canteens, webbed belts, boots, tents, mess kits and rubberized ponchos, rusted machetes and trenching tools, all laid out on rickety tables and stacked up on metal shelving, up to the high ceiling where weak bulbs dangled from naked cords. Anything can be found in a store like that. Sometimes the quality is fine: reams of 24-pound rag paper; big old ledgers with creamy stock, wide margins, deckled edges and leather binding. I saw a display case stacked with cigar boxes, and asked the proprietor, who had come out now and stood there in baggy striped pants, a ravelled, wool cardigan of faded scarlet and silver—white-haired, pinkfaced, smoothshaven, and smoking a fine meerschaum on whose bowl a mermaid swam forward like a Naiad on the bowsprit of a clipper. I asked him if by some chance he had any vintage Habanos tucked away there? You never know. "No, nothing like that," he said puffing away rather contemptuously, I thought, even sneeringly. Well, what was in those fine Monte Cristo boxes? He reached down and handed me one: instead of Churchill Corona Coronas, it held shiny clips of neat copper and brass fingers, oiled 7.65 ammo. I see, I said. "So you do," he replied, taking the box and placing it back carefully with the others stacked up in the case. Would you perhaps have a good shotgun for me? "If you like, I might have something for you, yes." He turned towards the partition that divided the store. My wife frowned at me, but followed after.

We went round to the rear of the store. This part was much cleaner than the front: the floor waxed, the cabinets highly polished oak and walnut, their glass clear. In the middle of the floor stood a pair of .50 caliber machine guns on tripods, World War I types. They looked ready for use, belts of rounds draped out and folded in their metal boxes like metallic tripes. There were bazookas on fine old mahogany tables; there were grenade launchers, recoilless rocket guns, 200mm mortars, automatic cannons, a Bofors anti-aircraft gun. In the cases pistols of all sizes, and rifles in the cabinets, Brownings, Mausers, Mannlichers, M-1's, M-16's. My wife picked up a Kalashnikov assault rifle and hefted it. I turned the wavering muzzle away and said she ought to keep her finger off the trigger. "This is more like it," she said, cradling it under the crook of her arm like a guerrilla and sweeping in a circle. I said she should keep her fingers out of the trigger guard.

The proprietor stood up from behind the large case then. He'd been stooped over and fussing in a low drawer. He smiled wanly at me around the amber mouthpice of his pipe as he held out a large gun. "This is what I think you might be wanting, I think. Something extraordinary." I took it from him. It was an old shotgun, a make I didn't recognize. It was quite beautiful, and I said so. The stock was burl walnut; the breech of heavy silver, engraved all over with a forest of flowers and curvetting stags and leaping hounds; the barrels were blued to perfection, satiny, oiled; the trigger guard gilded and velvety to the touch. Perfectly balanced: it went up against my shoulder as though made for me. It broke apart at a touch: the action was almost liquid. "Traps, hunting, whatever you like with a weapon like this," he said, puffing away. I turned it about, just to enjoy the feel of it, and noticed a silver plate sunk in the heel of the stock. It had letters engraved in elaborated Gothic script. When I made them out I was surprised: entwined with minute patterns of stylized small game and oak leaves, the name was mine. What a coincidence!

The proprietor, who was watching my wife toying with the deadly, Russian automatic weapon, raised his eyebrows shaggily, but said nothing. Neither did he move to warn her himself or take it from her, though it made me uneasy, her behaving that way behind my back. She hated guns, so I thought she was being sardonic. I wanted her to look at this shotgun of mine. It's quite a coincidence! I said again. "I don't know," the proprietor finally replied, still watching her, "but we could find out, couldn't we." I only wish we could, I said.

He hauled out a great old record book then, dropped it down on the counter top, and began thumbing through it. It was like the registers you still see sometimes in some decrepit spa in Europe somewhere, full of names and numbers written in every kind of hand, splotched here and there, and glowing in the faded inks of all the colors of the rainbow. How old was that book? I wondered. The proprietor was in no hurry. He seemed to relish the chance to browse through it while I waited: I could see the pleasure he took in it, as though running over the pedigrees of fine old guns of the last two centuries reminded him of the very weapons themselves. That must be a rare catalogue, I said. All yours? "So it is," he said. "So they were." The paper was heavy, deckled; the early signatures were almost faded out or illegible with weevil holes. The latter third of the volume was, however, still unused, and the paper fresh as though it had been bound yesterday. Seems up to date, doesn't it. "Yes," he mumbled, running his arthritic and tobacco-stained finger down a column, the nails of that gnarled hand broken and black with dottle—he had a way of tamping the hot wad in his meerschaum down as though he couldn't even feel the fire of the glowing ember he puffed at. "Here we are," he said in a voice that showed no happiness in having found the record of this gun. A neutral voice, bored in fact. "There are only two others like it. This one has had but three owners since it was made...oh, about 1928 or 1929, I should imagine." Where does it come from? "It's a German make. Can't you see that?" He was sneering at me. I suppose so. Well, how did it get to America then? and how did it come to you, I said. I was almost shouting at him. Well?

He shrugged at me. He wasn't telling. He pointed at the names in the ledger again. I couldn't read them upside down, and all I could make out was that it had been sold three times. After the War, the space went blank. I'll buy it, of course. I had decided right there. "But can you afford an item like this after all?" he said, not to me but to my wife, as though she were the one to ask. I turned and held it out to her. Whatever it costs, I said, we're buying it. She tucked the light and dangerous Kalashnikov weapon under her arm again and stood there, legs apart, looking skeptically at me and my shotgun. I admitted the price seemed rather high. But, I said, the name on it was mine, too. And so.... "And so?" she said. That was my reason, I said. She demurred, "Strange, yes, but—" But nothing! The point is, who's that original owner! How did he come to have my name!

She wasn't listening. The proprietor had stepped round me. He was putting the leather strap of that Kalashnikov over her shoulder. He was showing her how to release the safety catch. She followed his bony fingers with her long, soft ones. My own voice sounded dim in my ears, so long ago, and faraway.

AFRODITE

BECAUSE it was high summer in the Mohawk Valley, and the tumult of July's thunderbolt-riddled days had passed, I meditated in peace in my study on the second floor of the Greek Revival house we lived in, built long ago in the early 19th century, and rebuilt again in the 1950's into two apartments. The downstairs place was inhabited meagerly by Gertrude and David and their boys, all off camping in some gulch at the bottom of the Grand Canyon, he tapping at two-billion-year-old strata for specimens of proof for his geology classes, she wrinkling deeper into what she'd become, angular, hollowchested, confused, the boys wallowing in the Red Colorado River clay, hardening into spasmodic sticks. It was peaceful now without their tromping and bellowing below. The paperweight on my desk was a big fossil scallop shell he'd brought back three years ago as a souvenir of the times when Arizona had lain beneath the foaming waves of archaic seas.

Now the ghosts of the two old spinsters, last of their line, to whom this house had belonged once, could ascend from the earthen-floored cellar and stump through their apartment, as they never cared to do when the Crawleys were home during the academic year, perhaps preferring to wander about fretting, or to squat beside the washers and dryers on the south side where gelid sunlight lit the muddy panes cut in the foundation wall, offering them a little cold comfort. We preferred it like that too: our little boy had seen the sisters in his room one evening and screamed from his crib, pointing over my shoulder as I soothed him, telling them to go away, go away.... More than once I'd been aroused from sleep as they paced down the long hallway of our apartment, making faint, shoe-creaking sounds, not on the floorboards, and raising the hairs of my body like the spicules of a sea urchin. My wife never woke, though. Her name is the same as the younger of the sisters. When they passed through the rooms they'd occupied for nearly ninety years, even the squirrels in the vast attic above us ceased their midnight gambols, and stopped trickling their acorns down inside the thick walls. In summer, though, they took some light and air in the Crawleys' place, and never disturbed us at all. It was a compromise: I had asked them, out loud, to stay out of the children's rooms, since it was no good for little ones to be scared by old ladies who aren't there. Keep to the Crawleys', I implored the empty air, you can share the space with their bodies, they won't even notice you, and so keep from troubling our wits! That was a reasonable request, I thought, since we paid rent to the College, not to them. And that was that.

All morning I'd been meditating in my study under the front gable, shaded by the canopy of great, ancient elms surrounding the house. It was quiet across the road: the fraternity houses were shut down for the summer. So was the home of Ulysses S. Grant's daughter, she having died last winter at eighty-eight. Robins hopping on the lawns, heads cocked for grubs, the jays fighting around as usual, the wren tending her tiny nest, flitting in and out of the eave like a blur in one's vision, cardinals, orioles and doves visiting through the morning hours. My wife was out back under the apple tree in the garden with the children. Occasionally a pickup rattling by on the cobbled road, and a cow lowing far down in the valley. The cicadas of August tuning up for the afternoon's tedious static.

Meditating, if it can be termed that, sitting two hours looking out at lawns, the road, the old white houses behind their hedges on the other side. I'd come to realize that somehow, somewhere, I had lost my self. I had no idea where to look now. Yet it waited for me. Nearby, perhaps. Or far off. But not here. We'd parted one day without even a farewell, like former friends at a crossing, and gone our separate ways. And here I am, thirty. The road I'd taken had come abruptly to an end. No track led on from it now. Must I go back all that way to the fork? Then what? I might go on, always hoping to catch up, and knowing time lost is lost forever, like myself. So I sit here at this roadside in the Mohawk Valley. And wait, wondering how to proceed. It has been three years now. No one, it seems, can tell you. You are alone. Absolutely. My meditation this morning says simply, It's useless for an object to seek the subject which it is. Only the subject could seek, and the subject cannot find itself by seeking. Because what's sought is necessarily elsewhere than that which seeks it. The sought-for is in a different moment of time, and in a different region of space, from those moments of time and space occupied by that which is seeking. If you could have it, you wouldn't be seeking it. Seeking it, yourself, is vain. It can be presented to you though. How? and by whom? It depends.

I got up feeling the booklined walls of my little study closing on me as if to blot me out, in the way I had just obliterated a gnat by closing my fist. Queenie, our golden retriever, got up with me. I went down the stairs and stepped out on the verandah. It was nearly noon. Beyond the shade of the elms, the sun floated swelling up to its height. I crossed the lawn and walked up College Road to the Grant house, slipped through the garden and went out back into a copse that shielded it from the winter gales, walked down the path that dipped through among those trees, and climbed again to the pastures running beside an old apple orchard that spread out along the crown of the long hill heading away from the College. This hill was a ridge stretching ten miles north and south, paralleled by similar rolling hills to the east and the west. I was walking southwards through the old pastures. Here and there the mounded green grass was mined by groundhogs and rabbits, and cropped by horses some faculty kept. In the springtime, cows from the adjacent dairy farms were let out here to forage after the long months of silage. There were always crops of common field mushrooms battening on the manure, and giant puffballs, white as bleached skulls. Last week's rain had brought them out, and I could see many "Yoricks," as we called them, lying here and there where they'd popped from the ground. I regretted having left the basket on the porch.

No shade out here, and no breeze now. To my right, the apple trees, full of small green fruit. On my left, a pair of horses standing side by side at the barbed wire, head to rump, switching the flies from one another's face. About a half-mile ahead, the woods I was making for: a tall, second-growth forest in which you could escape the sun to rest beneath the shadowing alders and beeches, breathing in the tang of rotted log and leaf-mold and ferns, where trillium sprouted in lavender and white choruses. In this wood, there were no directions: the sun scatters into a diffuse greeny light filtering through the thick layer of branches, and only the faintly traced path winds through to come out nowhere...down a narrow ravine where a brook flows clotted with green slime. Wild grape covers that deep ditch and its slopes, and not much else but sumac and poison oak. Swarms of midges and mosquitos hang over it. In this wood it is always silent, except for the rasping of a crow floating between the tall, thin treeboles. Sometimes a pair of phoebes calls sweetly in the depths, echoing. But not disturbing the heavy stillness. In there, misery is assuaged for an hour. And, emerging afterward by the same path you have taken in, you are even glad to be back in the empty light once more on the meadows and pastureland, and heading somewhere again, home perhaps, with a few huckleberries and blackberries garnered along the way and staining your hands blue. A palliative, if no remedy.

As I looked along the track and the wall of that wood ahead, I felt the midday light glancing about at violent angles, and not just pouring down over the fields. I blinked at the strange, invisible shafts flickering around me. The ground seemed suddenly to be thrumming, a sound louder than the usual buzz and hum of the bees hovering over the clover and the daisies, milkweed and Queen Anne's Lace. A low susurration, and behind it a muffled low roaring that seemed to rise out of the grass on which I walked. The ground of the faint track seemed springy, elastic, a thick carpet spread upon a lake. As though there were no flinty granite beneath but a dark, and a warm, sea, and I was treading on matted weed. Dizzied, I kept on going. There is solid world here, I said to myself, plain, simple, poor, meagerly alive, but solid.

The yelping of the bitch stopped me. She was poised up ahead, alert, her tail stiff and high. She scented something. Then she began coursing back and forth, her nose to the track. I saw what her nose was thrilled by: just before the gate into the forest, right in the middle of the way, a great, ten-point buck faced us, his antlers lifted high. The bitch hadn't seen him. She kept her nose to the ground she was eagerly traversing. The buck watched her coming. He also gazed at me where I stood, his ears flicking. No one had ever brought down such grand game in these parts, where there's not enough forage or cover for the likes of that stranger. I watched Queenie as she began running toward him; he stood his ground watching me. Then she lifted her muzzle and saw him too. With a crazy, strangled bark, she rushed him. Casually the stag turned, his head twisted back to keep me in his view, and snapped his white rump, bounding away into the dark wood, the retriever in wild pursuit. I called out to her; it was useless. I could hear her baying fade into the echoing forest, fainting away as the buck led her off in chase. That fool might never find her way back. Nothing to be done now.

I kept on anyway. As I neared the spot, I saw that the dried grasses were crushed near the track. The stag had bedded down here. I stopped to pick up a clump of coarse red hairs snagged on a twist of briar beside his couch. The sunlight flooded down terribly then, as if a boiling cauldron had been tipped out overhead from the zenith. The roaring low rolling hum out of the earth grew until it sounded like surf thundering in. What was this? I swayed. I felt myself being forced down, the ground coming up for me. I yielded: I dropped to my knees for the first time in my life. Something was sweeping at me. The air split apart before its progress. What I felt was the pressure of its coming. I couldn't look up from the earth. I stared at the stag's lair, the tangled grasses and the tiny purple clover and daisies enmeshed among the broken stalks. The space about me was thickening with light and heat. It drummed. Far off, I heard the last belling of that maddened bitch, down and over the little valley to the west it seemed, miles off now.

And I knew what it was.

Afrodite! I shouted that name. At the same instant I was flung on my face. I did not dare to look up. Calmly I lay there, thinking, This is extraordinary: you have not sought this: neither have you deserved this: yet it has come: there is no remorse, no panic: she is there: there is only joy: brilliant joy: it will not stay: be thankful. Laughing and mumbling tears, full of a gratitude I had not known was in me to offer, I gave thanks. I called out to this bombarding passage of light and immense heat—this noise and power erupting from the earth and pouring like a wind over me, and passing steadily by like a great vessel—Afrodite! Io, Afrodite!

When I returned some hours later, my wife sat on the verandah, rocking the child in her lap. A glass of sherry was in her hand, the bottle at her feet. She smiled at me, reaching up to tug a straw from my hair.

Queenie came home the next day, matted with mud, her tawny coat a mass of burrs, her pads swollen and bleeding, her chest caved-in, brokenwinded. She drank her fill, and stretched out to sleep for a whole day and night.

CORINTH

AFTER A TIME on the wagon things got better, despite the drought. The first months seemed even good, I thought. Or good enough. I'd returned to my old friend for some repair work on the analysis, and after nine months I saw that there was no table I couldn't drink myself under. Now I knew that even the one single martini before dinner heralded brandies till midnight, sleeplessness, and empty dreams. For the past seven years things had gone very well with me, I thought. Or well enough. So when like most good things it ended abruptly, I was rather startled. It had all been delusion. Yet receptions, parties, dinners, business conferences and luncheons, and just plain friendly occasions for boozing still come remorselessly along in the ritual round of the calendar. I take soda water now: I ride on the wagon up high. It is, after all, a desert that stretches only as far as the horizon, though that's as far as one can see each morning. What lies beyond, we don't know until we get there.

Christmas week: surprise party for the twenty-fifth anniversary of our nuptials. The door's opened wide to us by her parents, smiling, beyond their golden celebration:

patient, quiet, all quarrels done with. The parcels, all holding silver things for us, are hidden behind the Chinese screen, with its phoenix and dragon flitting forever through a mountain mist somewhere: a tea service, a carving set, salt & pepper made of antique heavy Russian silver, cruets, wine goblets, an old heavy tray of high relief showing in the playful manner of Fragonard a pair of mature, naked lovers coming together beneath an oak tree; a coffee urn, a pair of richly-carved seven-branched candelabra, an ornate empty picture frame. And finally a silver nymph, her arms held out before her, offering a laurel wreath. She stands on tiptoe upon a radiator cap, and will replace the chromed steel three-armed star on the hood of her Mercedes. I sit with my iced sodawater at one end of the long dinner table; at the other end, she grows gay with the heavy, sharp Burgundy, boisterous, rather giddy.

On her right hand she's placed José, our fosterling. José Mendez is a handsome boy of nineteen from New York, a Costa Rican kid who's been shipped west on our recognizance. Oldest of thirteen, father locked up for life in Attica on a junk-pushing conviction, mother struggling vainly to keep the two next ones, girls, off the street and slaving honestly behind sewing machines in the garment district to support her and the rest of her tribe. José had been slipping into trouble, despite his clubbed foot. War Minister though he was for the Delphians, he didn't want any part of that short, desperate life of the gangs up there in East Harlem. He'd already shown prowess with the machete, against some hapless Thebans; so said the whitebearded social worker who'd shepherded him our way. Now he was gainfully employed in San Marino here, a bagboy at the Alpha Beta Market. Nights he worked at his remaining highschool courses, doing other chores for us around the place at odd hours as well. A clever boy, José, quickly fitting with no difficulty into our big, empty house, which must feel like a palace to him. Three swift months pass, and she was doting on him. José this, José that, in every sentence, José. Her new son.

Perhaps he is part of the reason I'd finally quit. Perhaps not. There were those ten years when we'd been busy establishing ourselves; seven when I'd refused; seven she, afraid of her age. Yet here we are with a grown son. And there she sits at the other end of the sumptuous board, with its thick padded linen, stiff napkins, sparkling crystal, good vintages, and a succession of festive dishes four of our oldest friends carry in triumphantly. Laughter, gay talk. No one hears much amidst the chatter and music. But I can hear everything she says down at her end, as though we were alone. Next year José is to have her Mercedes, with its new silver radiator cap. When he marries, José shall have our silver. José is going to go to a college nearby, so she will have her eye on him. José's a golfer. José sits his horse like a hidalgo. Girlish giggles, her hand reaching out quite unconsciously to squeeze the boy's, or to stroke and pat his shoulder. Exhilarant with wine, her eyes filling with fond tears, affection rampant in them; her rounded dove's breasts puffing up in that lowcut white gown; the emeralds in her small earshells setting off her wide, green eyes wonderfully, eyes that appear blind to me, unseeing, as twenty-five childless years brim over with tenderness. José is abashed by this demonstration: the handsome, reticent fellow turns to glance at me, he smiles shyly as if to beg my pardon for her extravagance. Where he got such good manners from, I don't know. Not up in East Harlem among the warring gangs. Even TV could never have revealed to him how we really live here in San Marino, this paradise of stockbrokers, executives, lawyers and doctors below the San Gabriel Mountains, just east of

Los Angeles beside the Santa Anita track. He's adapted very well, I think. Or well enough. How many years has it been since I sensed that moist heat fulminant between her thighs, making her restless in her seat: from my end of the long table she seems a bird bobbing on its perch. Well, well. But our old friends, and her own parents, show me visibly that they notice nothing, nothing at all as she exhibits her foster son and herself to them like this, even though no papers of domiciliation have been signed as yet during this trial period.

Next, New Year. She is Chairlady of the San Marino Rose Bowl Parade Float Committee, working till dawn the last three nights, supervising the team of twelve women decorating our entry with 500,000 chrysanthemum blossoms. This year the theme is World of Mystery, and she's designed our sixty-foot float: GOLD COAST. The long platform has a sort of magic isle, with a bower, surrounded by flowing waters. Miss San Marino's a nymph nearly naked in the chill of New Year's morning. Servant boys in flower-printed loincloths bring her tribute, among whom is José looking like Ariel, only lacking the butterfly wings: a gilt tiara glints with rhinestones on his curly head, gold dust flows from his body. San Marino wins Honorary Mention for Original Concept. The blue ribbon is laid away that evening in the desk drawer somewhere.

Thus in brilliant fancy we enter our twenty-sixth year. Others will come, although I cannot see them now. This week has been enough. It seems there are other ways to make a lot of money easily besides expanding real estate holdings. The lengthy board meeting this afternoon proves that, if I need proof. I had opposed the Corporation's use of venture capital, no matter how high the interest and fast the turnover, for the support of certain kinds of publishing: namely the glossy magazines for men and women spreading everywhere these days, those featuring ten to twenty-five pages of photographic collections in full color. Picture stories of naked young people in various postures of genital display, pantomiming the erotic. Mostly girls, however, viewed close up through soft fuzzed light, pudenda opened, engorged and glistening, or stroked by their own amorous fingers, the nails long and painted, the limbs and torso propped at angles impossible to sustain steadily or long in our gravity, except for such still-life portraiture. Twenty pages of Letters to the Editor, all written in the one style of schoolyard porn, summarizing incredible escapades in that monotonous prose, and offering imaginary climaxes in which the one thing inaccessible to language is declared: the sense of the act of union. With another person or thing. Or perhaps even with oneself. But the board graphed our activity, and the bottom line is clear: we'd loaned out $10 million last year to three different magazines with a gross, combined circulation of twelve million copies, meaning up to forty million readers—and we had recouped nearly half of our principal in interest charges alone! Nice work if you can get it. I am surprised a staid bank like ours derives such pleasure from loansharking. Of course, we'd borrowed most of this capital from a friend of the Chairman of the Board. It should be as obvious to the examiners as it is to me that we're being used as the conduit for money with a higher than normal temperature, neutral green to the touch though it seems. Examiners are not concerned with the pathology of our money yet: the ethical thermometer has not been patented that might reveal a problem here. I had thought I was the manager in charge of the Loan Division. During all these years I'd believed I had independent powers of decision, and could run things as I liked. As with so many other matters, it turns out I have no such powers.

Exasperated at my helplessness in the face of that bottom line—the chart's carried round the table, and whoever saw a profits graph pointing up at 45 degrees—what I finally remarked at the board meeting, about cabbage and cunt, though meant to be comical, seemed to me tragic. Money is the only oracle. When it begins to talk, the best, the proper thing is silence.

That board meeting over sooner than usual, I make for home early. The printouts will be stacked neatly folded on my desk Monday morning, and I shall initial them: OK OK OK.... I leave my chariot for servicing at our garage six blocks down from Alma Real. And home I stroll, thoughtful. Below me to the west, vaguely visible in the depths of a heavy sulfurbrown lake of smog lies Los Angeles. That slowly undulant swamp of polluted air is drifting by just below San Marino towards the east, to slosh through the pass and spread out over the hundreds of square miles of citrus and avocado groves of Riverside County too, its fringes lapping now at Palm Springs far out in the desert, and its topmost froth withering the tall pines atop the peaks of Big Bear Mountain, Mount Baldy and Arrowhead. If this inversion persists another day, it will accumulate and pour up over us here in San Marino. The sun of late afternoon's already coppery; it will glow scarlet and burn invisibly away as it descends through the smog into the ocean beyond. Only a few months during the winter weeks do we see it set in the Pacific from here, if we're lucky. Yet our lawns and gardens sparkle freshly, and all kinds of exotic trees, flowers and plants flourish around these houses. It seems pleasant to walk home, even if it's uphill all the way on Alma Real. I carry my coat, my sleeves are rolled, my tie loosened.

I am not thinking of money. Nor am I thinking about the three-dozen odd numbers of the magazines strewn over the conference table for our considered inspection, not merely to lie there exposed but also to remind the Board that important novelists, significant social philosophers, even scientists and highranking national polticians supply the texts for much of the printed matter distributed in columns between the ads for clothing, cars, deluxe furnishings, high fidelity components and other esoteric gadgetry. The Board can see, and know, if it wishes, how the emergent American mind is serviced by these slick organs: everything from yoga and Benin bronzes to Linear B and Sanskrit epics goes to support the Consumer Index through the medium of sensuality. I am thinking instead about comedy and tragedy, trying to remember what distinguished them from each other. Something about fate and failure, I think. And something about escaping fate after all. Could it be simply the difference between failure and success? Which was more interesting? Or, more true? I recall objecting once, It's hard to know, if you are in the drama, which kind of drama it is. They laughed at me because the prof said cuttingly, "You are not in the play, Mr. King, not ever. The play is played for you—so that you will see, and in the end know." It's the same thing in the end, it seems to me, I replied. "So it may seem to you, Mr. King. But things are seldom what they seem. Class?" And the class chorused, laughing at me, "Things are seldom what they seem!" So much for literature. Yet here am I, half my lifetime later, murmuring to myself that I should like to review the matter, just one more time.

José and Miss San Marino have been dating steadily since they rode the float up Orange Avenue to the Rose Bowl on New Year's Day. She's a bright-eyed girl, tall, with heavy, silky, black tresses flowing to her hips. Yolanda Graves. Father's a plumber just down the slope of the mountain, in South Pasadena. Oval black eyes, wide and liquid; long, fine nose; full, plumdark lips; willowy, with narrow and long breasts coming out to twin cones. Taller than any of us, and clever too, for a girl in the Rose Bowl category. Admitted to Stanford last year, and claims she's studying Astronautics. I see her straightening up alongside her ivory convertible XJ V-12 Jaguar across the road. Crossing to our home, she smiles down at me, radiant-toothed: the polished, slanting cheekbones seem to glint in the afternoon light like scars: she walks with dignity, a mahogany idol. We meet at the front walk. A surprise visit: she wants to take José out tonight. Before we go in, I ask Yolanda what she thinks is the difference between tragedy and comedy. Or don't such questions come up for a person majoring in Astronautics? "Oh, Mr. King, naturally," she says in that whispering contralto voice that holds reserve powers beneath the curving clavicles that dress her wide shoulders. "Only, we don't use those terms anymore today." Oh? I say, opening the door quietly to let her in.

The house is cool, still. The finches flick about and chirp in their wicker cage; the parrots chat burbling to one another in their brass cage. The airconditioning is the endless sighing, barely audible, of a sleeping giant, and through it comes the burr of the pumps for the big saltwater aquarium embedded in the wall separating us from the livingroom area and the other wings of the house. I like my collection of saltwater creatures—fish, molluscs, arthropods, anemones, sea horses. They stay put; they drift with grace through this imagined habitat; they demand no loving care, and acknowledge none that they are given, neither seeing nor knowing the terms of their existence here. And if they did, they could not understand.

"Those are really outdated ways of looking at drama," Yolanda continues as we go to the bar and pour ourselves long glasses of quinine soda with slices of lime. Really?

"You see, Mr. King, that whole complicated business of dancing around in horned masks and goatskins and all, and sacrificing someone, with everyone laughing and weeping and singing—that's all too primitive. We call drama today by different names. We call it irony, and resistance."

Irony, and resistance? Interesting. But don't you think, I say to this heifer-eyed, subtly made-up young woman, who is puckering her caterpillar-smooth eyebrows and pursing her full, purplish lips with abstract concentration as we sip our drinks and pace about the thick, peach Chinese rug covering the shining black slate floor, she in her silver sandals and shimmering in that slippery red synthetic sheath, her wide bronzebrown shoulders cut by the thinnest of strings—I can see she wears nothing beneath that dress—don't you think, Yolanda, that those terms are too restrictive? Human affairs aren't that limited. Surely, irony, and resistance do not suffice to describe the great plays in our repertoire? "That's all right, sir," she responds kindly, taking my arm unselfconsciously, as though I escorted her, and repeating, "Irony, and resistance. They are what we'll have to use from now on."

Well, it makes some sense, I admit. Given the way things are for us. But suppose— "You just think about it some more, Mr. King." She presses my arm, her hard young breast laid against it, quite unconsciously. Such as this are the girls in the glossies: chemists, computer technicians, psychologists, majors in Astronautics. The categories have changed, I suppose.

Conversing amiably, we have arrived at the wide threshold of our bedroom. Where we halt, side by side, rigid, and silenced.

On our bed there are two figures. José, dark as teak, fineboned and with supple muscle articulation over limbs and trunk, lies on his back, supine. The soles of his feet are dark brown, the left one twisted, knotted. His penis is erect; it is thick and long. His balls are tight, furred with hair as wiry as his own head of black curls. His penis pulses slowly, his left hand at its base gently holding it to point up at 45 degrees.

Beside him on all fours, my wife. Her blond hair down and dishevelled, damply matted, her smooth pale skin contrasting with José's flat brown. The dark blue veins of her thighs are traced miraculously as in marble columns. Her nails are polished vermilion, glowing with a wet fluorescence. On her fourth finger, the big diamond glittering even in the dimness of this room. She has lifted her leg in the air. She is about to cross it over his thighs to mount him. Her dense breasts swag from her round chest. Her butt waggles teasingly up and away from him. A pink, soft and pearly O, her anus. From this angle, she seems twenty years younger. Her woolly, darkblonde shag is visible in her crotch, a tuft of it thrusts out behind, almost a little tail.

José looks away from her towards us standing in the doorway. Surprised by his glance, frozen as she kneels above him, my wife looks back over her left shoulder. José does not move. His face is calm.

I'm sorry, I say. I don't mean to spoil your pleasure. No, no, please. Do go on.

Still, they do not move. They seem to hesitate, embarrassed. I step back, gripping Yolanda by her right elbow.

I lead Yolanda away. She is pensive, her eyes shaded. She's breathing short and hard. I take the glass of quinine soda and lime from her hand. I open the front door and she walks out to the street, her sandals slapping on the brick path. Then I shut the door carefully again.

IOCASTA

LONG DAY. Dossiers requiring my approval before going out over the Telex to managers of district stations around the country for last-minute action during the weekend. By Monday morning our campaign would be rolling, or we were lost. Market closed uncertainly, confused: bearish so far as I could tell, key indicators wobbling and menacing the week's gains. Where would the next rally develop, if at all? The spirit of contradiction rules us all now. Experts sitting on their hands while speculators slip in like sharks scattering the schools of little people. As well as scaring the great institutions who in the absence of reliable pointers are drawing in their ranks, conserving effort and resources as best they can. All day long I sensed weakening, a general loss of nerve originating not in the echelon of the leaders, as has occurred too often in the last hundred years, but lower down, at the base of the structure in fact. Plenty of prognosticators raising their voices now in a clamor of doom and destruction, just like licensed prophets. True, conditions are precipitating in which, given the presence onstage of certain characters at a certain hour, the result must be a panic. Not yet; but soon enough. In my own area, for instance, things suddenly started moving yesterday. Justice Department puts us on notice: subpoenas are flying our way: everyone in the organization who is anyone will be called in for questioning. Dismaying; sickening; saddening too: years and years of effort threatened by one man's astonishing suit! He'd spotted the very place in our entire elaboration where we could be attacked. He had bided his time; he had prepared his case with infinite detail, and was challenging us at the moment when our attention is devoted to international complexities and the domestic economy, which is now revealing signs of strain unfortunately so severe it can no longer be patched with temporary expedients. Were I writing the text, I think I should choose this very situation as the example of a classical case of catastrophe, for no virtuoso display of managerial expertise will carry us through the oncoming crisis unharmed. How much time is there? Anyone's merest guess. And now, now this one man's claim could bring heaven crashing on our heads. As though an old crippled fellow with a knobbly blackthorn stick wrenching at a crack in the wall were to cause the World Trade Center's 110 storeys to split, shatter, totter slowly and collapse in a mountain of rubble of marble and glass and steel flooding over Wall Street, spilling into the Hudson around the Battery, causing an eddying riptide and whirlpool to form and suck barges and tugs and ferries from their courses, pulling them down to disaster. Yet I know the World Trade Center cannot fall. I know we'll get beyond this situation too, because reality is not a dramatic episode in some chapter of the text, after all. Reality floats into the future on the imponderable. The Market will bottom out eventually, no matter how low its values have sunk: somewhere there's bedrock. Furthermore, I'll put our corps of lawyers to chorusing appeals on our case for years and years to come.

She called me away at midnight from the high windows that look out over the terrace, where a dozen potted trees stand shrouded in canvas: so many shapeless, featureless, dormant sentries. How long had I been standing there in my blue paisley silk robe, savoring my cigar and sipping the glass of whiskey as the warmth drained from the apartment...an hour? The great orb of the bonewhite wintry moon had already shrunk to a frozen, glaring disk as it flew up out of sight and hung somewhere before starting its decline in the West. But now from the zenith its harsh, blued brilliance fell in a wide swath rippling over the blackrunning tidal current of the East River. From up here that stream swirled past, impressing me as always with its living oily violence. Again she was calling to me from upstairs, and I turned, reluctant, suddenly tired, my mind turbid, humming with the crosstalk of my nerves. After the frenzy of this week past, even the orders I'd left at the close of day hadn't provided me with repose. It seemed to me in the stillness of this penthouse, sealed from the gusts of frigid wind scouring the walls and terraces up here like slashes of invisible blades, that my ears rang. The kind of tintinnabulation one cannot avoid hearing deep in the skull, as though a brace of shotguns at a trapshooting meet had been firing beside my ears for hours.

She sat erect in bed, drinking from her red, handblown glass tumbler: hot milk and honey laced with Spanish brandy. *Von Clausewitz on War.* A new edition, with commentary by some of our more intelligent political savants, to place the issue into our present perspective, wherever that is. At bedtime she likes history, and practical theory. I must settle for the dossiers: those raw numbers and the field reports I need to resolve before the next day's struggle. Even at bedtime I haven't leisure to reflect, although I am well aware that time is running

out—one must begin by amassing wisdom grain by grain,
and early on, as she had done. She's at it still. And how
gracefully she shares it with me, like her life. Without her, I
know, and well I know it, I should have come to nothing,
nothing at all.

"You look worn out, my darling," she says, lifting her
wide, slanted bluegreen eyes above the rims of her tiny,
tortoiseshell reading specs. I drop my robe and stretch out,
striking in slowmotion at floor and ceiling to unknot my
shoulders. I am, I laughed, utterly exhausted. "Then I'll let
you sleep for now. It will wait until morning, won't it." She
pats my pillow, swings the reading spotlight above over to
her side, and returns to *Clausewitz*. She would wake me as
the gray light edges the draperies with a ghostly, trembling
frame towards dawn: she would be pressed up against my
back, her long arms twined about me, her smooth, fine
fingers tracing invisible circles on my belly, the sharp nails
catching in my hair delicately, her firm, cool thigh thrown
lightly over my hip and sliding up and down, so that as I
rise heavily up from the deeps of slumber I'd sense pulsing
against my flank the hot breath of that secret creature
between her legs. For now I'd let go of the world, that faint
ringing persistent inside my head. I'd lapsed out as though
I had launched myself from a height and would drop,
floating and languourously flailing, and never to hit
bottom. The abyss, I remember thinking, cannot be fathomed. Is it because our time in the world is a stony narrow
ledge winding about a vast mountain? The base is obscured
by perpetual, shifting mists below. The summit lost in
light somewhere beyond our vision. The slope nearly
vertical, a sheer, gray, icy and sweating wall. We plod
ahead, upward, slowly and suffering, in single file on this
path for as long as we can, conversing brokenly, if we have
the fortitude, with the backs of those just before us, and

with the unseen faces of those just behind. Shouts, cries, snatches of echoing laughter, come like greetings occasionally from somewhere above, where the track must go round again ascending, or from below, where the others are making their own way climbing after us. How bleak, to think of it like this. It's enough to make one wish to revolt, to leap away in despair ... but then I recall those words— had I heard them spoken to me? *The abyss cannot be fathomed.*

Or was it the phone ringing that I'd thought I heard? Perhaps it had only begun to ring and she'd reached quickly out, as she always does, and lifted the receiver. I turned over, and returned to sleep. Or I tried to. The room was darkened now: only the nightlamp glowing dim on her side of the big bed. "Yes," she whispers into the mouthpiece gently and without alarm, as if she'd expected this caller in the middle of the night. A deep voice answers: it is an old man's slow, deep voice. Friend of hers. I know about him. She is close to him, and has been for very many years. He seems to be saying, low yet distinct, "I couldn't sleep tonight. Will you talk to me awhile. It's so painful."

And propping her pillow behind her, she replies, sliding up to a sitting position and lighting a cigarette—I could hear the click of the lighter's cover, the pop of the flame as the quartz flint ticked, I could smell the acrid butane fluid, and feel her ribcase expand as she drew the first puff deep into her lungs—and settling herself for a long talk through the darkest hour of this long winter's night. "It's all right," she croons in her throaty voice, "he's asleep, poor thing. The trouble out there's terrible. A week of siege. The fighting's tired him so. This is the first setback he's had. Maybe he'll make it. Maybe he won't. He needs rest now."

I pretend to be sleeping as she goes on. "No, he doesn't

know yet." I can hear his voice rumbling in the earpiece she must have propped on her shoulder in the way she has, so that she can hold the ashtray on her lap and smoke with the other hand. "Don't talk like that. It's not your fault, my darling. I've done what I can. You know that. But of course you are loved." I can't make out what he's saying as he goes on and on, like a man lost in drink or sorrow. I try hard to listen. My own heavy breathing, the deep respiration of the unconsciousness I am feigning, obscures his words to me. The tones come through, though: hoarse, growling, a distant desperation. As their conversation rambles on and they exchange sentences, then phrases, then intimate keywords, it is as if he were yet her lover from long, long ago. As if they'd remained friends all this time during our marriage, meeting for luncheon dates, calling one another for news, counsel, consolation, attending afternoon concerts and strolling through exhibits, sharing a profound and vivid relationship that is as important to her as . . . anything else. But it's her affair, not mine. It doesn't offend me, or annoy me. Nevertheless the secret endearments she whispers to him as she hears his story, cajoling his awful misery, promising him more and better days, reviewing the past, marking out the future . . . this side of the hushed, halfhidden talk makes me a little jealous. On principle. Simply, impersonally, so to speak. But not jealous of him. I know her. And I believe I know myself. Trust is all. And I trust. I try to keep awake, wondering what they are really talking of, as her voice sinks away, as she goes on listening to his ruminations, broken by endless pauses, it seems to me, in which she lights cigarette after cigarette, responding with sibilant ejaculations, "No, I can't . . . Saturday . . . Tuesday's better . . . I'll try to come . . . well yes, two, the opening . . . but of course, my darling one . . . I do . . . you know I've always . . . dearest, you mustn't go on so . . . you must believe what I tell you ... always there ... no, you're not alone in this ... please, you're making me so unhappy, my precious one ... truly, truly ... you're hurting yourself ... it's always been true, and ... we know it ... dear, dearest heart. ... " And still that voice continuing, distant, patient, droning and winding incomprehensibly this way and that, and deeper, yet farther off—she must have changed the earpiece to the other side. I wish she would speak in fuller sentences, so that I might follow their consultation. Yet even though she believes I am sleeping, she goes on answering with the guarded snatches one uses in the presence of the third person. It is something terribly important, I have realized. But what, and to whom?

I wanted to turn over, to seem to come surfacing for a moment from the depth, as if I'd been disturbed by them. Yet I found I couldn't move; I couldn't keep awake; I couldn't concentrate on her soft voice or on that man's indistinct words. Was it a dream, or did I imagine I finally heard, with the remnant of my futile effort to cling to a crumbling handhold of consciousness, the quiet clap of the receiver being cradled, the scribbling of the last cigarette stub in the ashtray, her long, shivering sigh as she turned her pillow down again and slid beneath the comforter, the chilled soles of her feet pressing against my calves as she prepared to plunge into her own sleep? Perhaps I recall thinking at last, She's still here. But where am I?

TELEMACHOS

JANUARY, and United Sporting goods advertises its annual inventory clearance sale. Items from last Fall's hunting season too. I am not a hunter, but it might be fun to practice archery in my own backyard.

I found a heavy, double-reflex Bear bow marked down 60%. Its original list price was far too high for me, unless it were taken and used seriously. I could afford it now, though. When I asked what the double XX branded into the grip meant, the salesman replied that it was a Second. Why? "Must be some slight defect in the finish somewhere, something you wouldn't notice anyway. It's guaranteed, otherwise." We turned it about, looking for the flaw that had not passed inspection. Finally, we decided that it must be that discoloration in the varnish just beneath the grip, and wouldn't be distracting. "You could scratch it like that yourself the very first day in the woods," he said. Yes, I could, but it would be my scratch and not someone else's wouldn't it? "Take it or leave it. But if you want it, it's yours for good. As is." He walked off, impatient, and began hanging ladies' tennis dresses on a rack. I took it, as is, at 60% off list. I had to. I could also pick up arrows, targets, a straw butt, forearm and finger guards and a couple of first-quality bowstrings, and still come out cheap, and be ready for practice as soon as I got home.

It was late afternoon when I had set everything up, exhilarated and eager to begin shooting. The shadows were thickening everywhere; the sun was low in the southwest over the purpled Pacific and the sailboats were clustering at the breakwater down at the marina, heading back to their berths as fast as they could before the early January nightfall. It was very quiet, no wind at all, and only the screech of a bluejay on the naked branch of the fig tree in the middle of the garden broke the calmness of the dusk.

I strapped the guard to my left forearm, slipped the finger gloves on my right hand, placed the heavy, longish bow behind my left calf and bent it with all my might, which was hardly enough, I found, to slip the loop of the bowstring over the top catch. It took me three tries, at that, and I was panting and beginning to sweat and tremble in my knees. This might prove embarrassing, I felt. I twanged the taut bowstring at my ear a few times while I rested and calmed my breathing. The tone was low and strong, and the bow now looked very handsome. Perhaps a 56-pound pull was a bit much for home purposes? Were I out for bear or elk, it might be right, but in my own back yard? Though if I didn't work at that heavy pull now, how could I draw the bow later in the woods?

I set one of the fine, long aluminum arrows into the handgrip, and, after touching the rough plastic feathers, I notched it. I placed my feet, took a deep breath, and swung the bow up to the correct position as I drew the string hard, all the way back to my right ear, and then—the bow broke in half in my hands! Was I then that strong? Or did that imperfection in the finish conceal a deep, fundamental flaw in the heartwood itself? Had I been cheated? It was branded a Second, yes. But it should have given me the same service as a new and perfect bow! I was angry. How could I prove the defect to have been in the bow, and not my powerful drawing of it? Perhaps I could glue it together again at the clean break, with one of the new epoxy resins, say? If that new superglue held, would the bow be elastic? I doubted very much.

I stood there as the moon came out, full and silver, over my shoulder, in the east. The arrows lay in their quiver on my back; my hands, laced with leather for shooting, held the two useless halves out before me; the now slack bowstring hung to my toes. I found myself fuming as I looked at the empty target leaning against the garage door. Never, never would I take a Second again! Not from anyone! Tears of frustrated fury scalded my cheeks. There were no guarantees to be had in this world anymore! To hell with United Sporting Goods! And to hell with them all!

XANTHIPPE

A RIPE OLD AGE. Overripe, actually. Then rotting at the end. Which takes him three years, dimming with the glaucoma, one dismal feature of the syndrome of diabetic degeneration. The final year was an introductory tour of purgatory: first, a cluster of light strokes that set him down in his recliner more or less for good, the right side of his body numbed, speech slurred—and as he was accustomed to scolding and instructing his patient wife by the hour, it made his sarcasms pathetically funny, because even then he never let up, not seeming to hear the vile nonsense he uttered—and, second, the capillary breakdown and resultant loss of circulation in his legs (he was a tall man, even taller than I), until there was a gangrenous left foot, so that we had to have the thing amputated above the knee he liked to pound on for emphasis. Not that he regarded it as a punishment, not that tough, selfish old cock—not for him. But if his suffering was meant to be an installment on the big and everlasting debt he'd accumulated, he could charge a lot of it off to his wife and daughter before it came through for collection. They could stand it better after all, was the way he calculated. I suppose he would have liked having a grandchild, if not necessarily by me. My children were already grown and gone by the time I married his daughter. Which wasn't that awkward: I was fifty, yet young enough to have been his son. What he wouldn't recognize was his hold on his child: she was already forty-two, and still his baby girl. In her own mind too.

Ah, what a sexy, feverish, hardworking and learned broad. A worshipper of bookish systems: philology, lost medieval Latin poets, iconography (frames and flowers, the headgear of various kinds of guildmembers in woodcuts or illuminated manuscripts and miniatures or incunabula, carvings on capitals in Romanesque basilicas or English pews, women's footgear, ditto, and Mongolian and Siberian folklore, with a concentration on fertility magic and motifs). Every year she changed the color of her hair, though her eyebrows and sporran stayed black and thick. Adorably nearsighted, she's always dropping one or the other contact lens. Nothing slows her down.

He did, though, at the end. I forebore pointing out that she was possessed, and obsessed by him. That he was her mother's responsibility surely. "My mother is incompetent. She always has been." Don't you want a child? I'd inquired on each birthday. "It's unnecessary—I still have him." What an admirable sense of reality she had, I thought.

He came through the amputation, reduced but much the same anyway. It ought to have made an impression on her. But she wore only that absorbed and anxiously vexed expression—a kind of reaction to time's passage, and mortality too—and I saw she'd failed to take the hint. What with tending him and her mother, her studies, her writing...she had found those means to stave off time for another year. Like father, like daughter: both refused to practice death. "Do you love me?" she would whisper hoarsely, sliding her chilled legs under the comforter past midnight, stretching her long cold form against my back after coming in late from their frantic evening with him, cheering him up, sustaining him by tremendous efforts of placation of every cranky whim, and rapt attention to his speeches against the clerisy, realtors, politicians and brokers. Especially the commodities men, because his chief means of making money was hampered now by increasing blindness: the room kept darkened from six a.m. on, as the lists of prices rolled up over the TV screen hour after hour and he studied his fluctuant fortune, hammering out numbers on his legal pad and pushing away at the buttons on the telephones beside him. While her mother changed the dressing on his missing limb, massaged his thighs, prepared his injections, washed his heavy torso and ministered to his flaring rages between calculations, bids, and conferences with the lawyer, the bank, and brokers in Chicago and New York. He might have done all that down in Palm Springs, which I suggested—but then his daughter wouldn't have been with him each evening till eleven, listening and regurgitating her day's findings in the libraries. Yes, I would say, I love you, thrilled awake by her marmoreal legs twining about me. And I'd have to show her then how very much I loved her, or she'd never get to sleep at all. Faithfully, I replenished what he'd drained away from her.

Something to consider philosophically, marriage. Unthinkable under any other kind of perspective. Worse, absurd. Marriage of course is fundamentally absurd. It is the beginning, not an end. A start, but no true goal. Yet— the start must be made. Something she could not even bring herself to imagine, let alone contemplate. When she was not working at her manuscripts, she went shopping with her girlfriends, as she termed them. I thought their taste flashy, and in Los Angeles that's saying something, since the good designers' clothes here are rather noisy, even when in the best taste. You'd never take her for a scholar, if you saw her slipping into her Corvette in Beverly Hills: you'd imagine her as the rather expensive property of someone dangerous in Las Vegas.

Three weeks ago, pressure from the world of the real began mounting. I sighed to see the harried look in her eyes become fixed in wan dismay. I said nothing. One can't, one must not argue with a wife. To have lifted that mask would have revealed another beneath it. One more heartrending: the face of fear. Under it would be the blankness of impending terror, terror mingled with remorse, a visage no artist has drawn—intellectual terror. And beneath that one would be yet another mask, the rigid one of sorrow, downcast and frozen. No need to be curious about these skindeep masks. Time would peel away each one, and in a very few days. I should see them all, one by one. And I was prepared, if she wasn't. Nevertheless, I was not ready for the last one, this face of unforgiving, sullen fury she wears against me now every day. Not that, on reflection, I mind. It's better having her vivid, hating me, than drifting off lost on the burning marl of despairing grief.

His end arrived as feared, though it had not been imagined. Reality seldom is. The toes on his other foot blackened. Back into the hospital. It was possibly either/or. It was probably both/and. All discussion was finally stopped: everything is subject to the dialectic, but death. Signs of heart failure. On the machine. Gangrene is slow, and could wait. He had some affairs to finish, so the broker came to visit as regularly as his household of wife, daughter, and Vye, their maid. I was present too; but he never saw me again. If ever he had. For a week everyone knew it was going to be over, though he didn't. He would not know. Be kind to him, I said. "I have been," she snapped back, "for forty-two years, and my back hurts." She'd been snapping and rolling her head around on her shoulders for months now, refusing to see a doctor, a masseur, or do anything for herself. "It's nerves, tension," she'd say, rolling her head about with pain, dementedly rolling it at meals, while driving, or reading.

Final day. Intensive care ward. Everything's hooked up, lights and oscilloscopes and graphs ticking and registering away. Nurse at the console, monitoring the dozen souls at her fingertips, flickering, hovering, hesitating on the thinnest margin between this place and the nowhere that is elsewhere. The broker has taken his last orders: porkbellies, soybeans, eggs, silver and gold, and coffee—options held back and exercised, but ten new options on coffee, at $7600 each... they will surely come in for a half million in six months or so, and may even cover the rest of his losses. He looks up at his daughter blindly, his hand groping in the air for hers—and missing, because she is trying just then to replace the contact lens her tears have washed out of place on her swollen black pupils. His empty palm falls on his groin with a spasmed jerk, and he's gone. Cardiac arrest at seventy-seven. Reasonably long career, after all. Enough's enough.

The rains have come, as they should in February. Inches sheeting down all day for days now, waves of rain dashing over the coast all night, sometimes pattering and sometimes bucketing and smashing over the roofs. For six years we have had very dry weather, a drought, fires and duststorms and dreary bright blazing months of bitter and polluted, oily-brown, smogfilled skies. Now the rains are washing the cities and deserts of Southern California clean, sweeping down the suburban hillsides in torrents of mud, flashfloods filled with cars and furniture and debris.

The streets glisten black, the air is cool and sweet once more. The trees are shining with all their varied greens and greenblues, the rich foliage that had lain buried under the dust of seasons of parching winds. Our cortege departs after the viewing and service. The cars pick their way ten miles through the steady downpour, arriving at last at Forest Lawn. The efficiency of the California funeral is expected; but on this day it is not to be had. And so the last mask of my wife, hidden till now under her raw face of heavy sorrow, comes to be exposed by what happens, a scene devised by some ruthless comedian.

I am the lead pallbearer, on the right. To my left, his broker. Behind me, his lawyer; to his left the CPA. Last, the manager of his bank, a nervous fellow whose working week had long been knotted up in his affairs more than was good for his career, or the branch of the bank; and to his left, the maid's husband, a tall, scar-faced man, with new, lavender bruises and cuts on his misshapen cheeks. His eyes are swollen and bloodshot: he's still shaking with the massive hangover he's had since the police picked him up yesterday. In fact, there is a steel chain around Sam's waist, and it's connected to the handcuff on the wrist of a Sheriff's Deputy who's trailing along behind him, blocking the way of the women, my wife and her mother, who should properly follow the casket but are forced to stumble after the officer. And behind them, hiding her puffy face, with its newly broken-off front teeth and swollen, broken nose and half-shut eyes, is their maid of twenty-five years' loyal service, Vye. His former cronies, speculators and gamblers, are all either dead, or in the VA Hospital, or at home, safe from this blinding rainstorm.

Out of respect for her employer, who was always good to her—until this past week—Vye has come. Otherwise, the hour he died she quit. The old man was also an inveterate handicapper, and Vye had placed his bets for him, avoiding wife and daughter by some system of signals they used between them. In the morning before he suddenly worsened and had to be shunted off into intensive care, he'd sent her out of the hospital room to lay a G-note on the nose of some mare running at Santa Anita with odds of 126-to-1 against her. She'd slipped him the message herself, a tip from a Mr. Zenophanes about that mudder. "'Yall put suthin on that nag youselfs,' thass what he tol me, sho he did. But I dint. Cos why? Cos marol man slaps my haid upside off for bettin you fatha's damn haystoves, stead of bringin home mah wages! If ah'd stop bettin, he'd cut drinkin. Po, yass, but quiet...till thother evenin!" She'd been too scared to put her hundred dollars on that horse—the old man's last words to her they'd been too, and good advice from the very porch of Hades. When that lady, Pythoness, sloshed in and paid off at 126-to-one, and she went on home in tears and told Sam, you can imagine how he took the news: the beating he'd given her before going out and blinding himself on gin was all too evident. Vye quit, and she was filing for divorce, too: she'd had Sam arrested, and then fetched him out of the tank to be an honorary pallbearer. Bail was $1000 and Vye had the money in one banknote out of my wife's purse: the book's runner delivered it at the door before we got in the car this morning, and she was toting that hundred grand or so right now, rolled up and wrapped in a fat rubberband. The lawyer'd someway gotten the Court to move fast, as a charity, and here was Sam and his guard. Poor man was sick and sore and angry all at once. And Vye meant what she said: my wife knew that her mother would be without her lifelong maid when she got home this afternoon. It would be a taste of hell.

The casket was slid out of the hearse, and we heaved it

aloft. The gravel road was washed out, and they'd stopped
the train of cars somewhere far enough from the gravesite
to give us a good walk through this drumming downpour.
After five paces we were ankle-deep in mud. But still we
came up to the hole in about ten minutes' trudging.
Lightning and monstrous thunders bashed about the San
Gabriels across the Valley, though we couldn't see them,
obscured as they were by the lowhanging, billowing,
grayblack clouds that rushed by from the Pacific twenty
miles to the west of us here on this slope. The priest had
read through more than half the burial service when a
messenger came splashing along from the front office: we
were gathered about the wrong hole in the ground. No
wonder there'd been none of the wreaths I'd expected to be
cluttering up the site. I had been thinking the florist's
truck had lost itself in some freeway tieup.

We got the coffin raised up again, after the grave-
diggers had jumped down into the soup to get their tapes
hooked under it once more. The machine they use these
days runs one way: it will winch a box down, but isn't
ratcheted or strong enough to haul one up again. Getting
hold on it now wasn't easy. The priest tried lending a hand,
and slipped face down into the side of the pit. We tugged
him up covered with red mud. All of us pallbearers slid and
struggled about trying to get it out and aloft. We were
running liquid mud from our armpits down. No one spoke a
word during this time: we grunted, fell, heaved and
stumbled about: our curses and choked-off exclamations
drowned in thunder and rain. Sam didn't move a finger, the
Sheriff's Deputy holding him on a short leash off to the
side, just to keep himself from being dragged down into the
crumbling hole with him.

In about three-quarters of an hour, we were finally at
the right excavation for my father-in-law, who seemed to

have grown heavier and heavier as we paced, falling off, now one, now another, on the detour the messenger took us on to find it in the rain. A miserable knot of people we were by then, coated with adobe-red mud, and soaked through, coats, hats, shoes: you would have imagined we'd emerged from a mining disaster. Heaps of flowers lay about our feet, ruined by the pelting rain, and the sky was quite black, even though it was just after noon. My wife held her mother up forcibly, her arms about her waist. "Get on with it, fool!" she hissed between her locked jaws. The priest was fumbling his breviary out of his pocket again, and I held a torn umbrella over his head as he thumbed for the service once again. Father, I whispered, forgive her, she doesn't know what she's doing. The old priest poked me sympathetically with his elbow as he began the prayers all over from the beginning. Listen, Padre, I muttered, let's have the shorter version this time, or we'll be drowned where we stand. I think we've had enough for one funeral already. He poked me again. I never looked up from beneath the rim of the umbrella at her on the other side of her father's grave as the priest ripped through the obsequies, skipping a halfdozen formulas and closing the affair with three breathless long sentences and amens. We scooped a few palmfuls of running mud down at the coffin, and turned away at last to try to find our way out of this field through the raging storm.

I tried taking her arm to keep her from slipping herself on the running, rutted gravel walks, but she shook me off fiercely. "You bastard," she said, "I'll never forgive you for this!" What had I done to her, I said, what was it now? Her mother said nothing, clinging to my left arm, staggering along, poor thing, panting and sobbing. "Don't worry, darling," she coughed at me, "the child's just upset."

"Upset? Shouldn't I be upset? He was disrespectful to

my father. He told the Father to skip almost the whole of the burial service and run us out of there. The whole thing's ruined. Is that a funeral? Let him go straight to hell!"

I tried taking her arm again, to keep her from stalking into a flowing puddle of water. No use. She stepped into it, heedless of the cold, fouled water that came halfway up her calves. She stood there, with her makeup streaked over her face, her copper hair straggling in glistening hanks over her cheeks, and she pointed her trembling, raging arm at me, weeping and growling at once: "You botched my father's funeral. I will never talk to you again!" I said nothing.

And she has not spoken to me since, though a year has passed. She may wish to; but she is proud. I hear her voice only in the darkness now, at midnight, when she grunts, face down, sometimes tearing at her pillow with her teeth as she lifts herself to take my thrusts, crying out, in vain, "Ah, ah—my god!"

MEDEA

IT SEEMED a good idea for her to travel this summer, and for me to stay at home for once. To my surprise I felt lazy, I'd had enough. Sleep, eat, play with the boys on the beach, catch up with my reading. Wednesdays we'd rent a boat and go fishing out in the Bay. Long summer evenings, cigars, playing through the record collection undisturbed. Restaurants; movies; in a word, relaxing. I've seen enough forts, enough statues, enough pictures and tombs; I'm tired of excavations and cenotaphs and the gabble of foreigners, always about money, if you listen to what they say. You can never bring anything back but yourself, and you're lucky not to get fleeced. In the end, it's all just menus and dysentery.

But she was happy to be launching off on her own. She's been angry, restless; the boys wore her down. Her girlfriends had set her up with this all-expenses-paid junket by recruiting her for a conference of psychoarchaeologists. Two weeks of papers and discussions by researchers from all over the globe: THE THRESHOLD—MAN, WOMAN, & PRIMAL PERCEPTION. She would pretend to collect their words and make them over into some kind of book. The money came from a Swede munitions tycoon who'd made his fortune selling armor-plate steel and guns to the Nazi Teutons, and was atoning by throwing exclusive seminars in his rebuilt tenth century Alpine schloss. I kissed her goodbye, wished her luck, and put her on Transworld's Flight #1 at noon. Already she looked gamesome, dressed for adventure: handsome, clear-eyed, fluttering free in her bright blue travelling suit.

After three weeks had passed without a card from her, I began to wonder if she were all right. The boys never thought about it; they were swimming, playing along the beach, reading comic books all day, and addling themselves with extra TV, staying up as long as they liked.

The fourth, then the fifth week passed. I had written to the schloss three times. No word came back. She must have been too busy. The conference was closing; she was due home after a week's sightseeing around Istanbul. This wasn't like her: she wrote messages of love loyally. Had something happened to her in Paris, at the schloss or, more likely, in Istanbul? I kept calm with the boys, who were asking when she was coming. They'd remembered they'd had a mother, I suppose. They were fed up with hamburgers and pizza and chop suey and sundaes, I suppose.

Seven weeks to the day, Transworld's Flight #3 landed on time at 11:11 p.m. The boys were asleep, I hoped, after the potion of warm cocoa I'd fed them. I stood at the arrival gate with a bunch of white carnations in my fist. And, yes, there she was, filing out with the three hundred dishevelled, worn tourists after a seventeen-hour hop from Turkey.

But how good she looked, fresher than the day she'd left me: tanned, thinner yet without seeming worn—except about the eyes, which were, I noted, ringed, hollow . . . but glowing with excitement, or passion. She wore a dress I'd never seen before: crimson, a silk brocade with green shadows of spirals visible in its luster.

I thrust my bunch of flowers out. She took them, reluctantly, her lips smiling, but only as with a faint memory of what her smile was. My stomach turned. She was here, safe; but something had changed. As we waited downstairs for her case to tumble from the chute, she took my shoulder, and gripped me hard with her left hand, half-turning away. "I have something to tell you," she said in a low voice, "so listen to me well." Did you have a good time? I asked. "Wonderful, but hectic." You're looking great, I said. "Thank you. And I feel great too."

The luggage came. I picked it up, and started for the exit. You must be tired out; you must feel like sleeping a week. "I do... but I won't." Well, till noon then. "I'm leaving at noon," she said.

I set the case down. My legs wouldn't move. "Flight #1 leaves at noon." May I ask where to? "I'm booked. I'm packing tonight." May I ask where to? She takes a deep breath; her face appears suddenly pitiless. The vacant terminal lobby, the late late hour, the long trip, the cruel fluorescent illumination? No, it's something in her.

"I met a man," she said. "I'm leaving. Everything's yours. The children too." I see, I said. I suppose I sounded utterly resigned. She expects resistance; she is prepared for bitterness, violence. Yet I know the inevitable, even before it comes. I always have. It's my gift. That's why I chose her. May I ask who he is? "Yes, of course. A wonderful man. About your age. I'm terribly in love with him. I don't know how it happened. I hardly recall how it happened. But it has been like being carried off by a tornado, for a month now. I can't live two days without him." Oh, I said. May I ask who he is?

She sighs, forlorn, as though reluctant to share even

that with me, so fully has she departed from our life into this new one of her own. "He's the Director of West German Television. A producer. A genius. Busy everywhere in the world. Rich. Handsome. Clever. Strong. He's taking me with him this week on his own yacht to film a terrific archaeological find. It's called the Argo." Ah, I said. "And we'll start our settlement: I don't need anything from you anymore. You'll keep the boys." Ah, I said. "And don't worry, you'll be taken care of too." How? I said. "I told him everything about you. He's very generous. He'll throw you a couple of scripts a year to write. You'll make out." Thanks, I said.

We got home at two a.m. She never woke the boys. She was in a quiet fury. She went right to the bedroom, opened all her drawers, and began laying out what she wanted, which was little enough—some fresh lingerie, a pair of shoes, a white suit. "He's waiting for me in Istanbul. You'll see to the paperwork here. No, no, don't touch me!"

Her mouth was set. There were tears in her eyes. But her mind was made up. She strode like a panther around our bedroom. And what is his name? I said.

"He's called Herr...." For the first time, she laughed, her skin flushed with warmth, her hands raised, opened with pleasure. And, as though daring me to smile, she cried out, "Herr Blumenpflanz!"

A THEBAN OSTRAKON

LATE THIS AFTERNOON I was dressing up to go round the corner to a cocktail party. It was a fundraiser for the maverick who's jumped two parties and is running as an Independent for senator. I don't care for his politics or rhetoric: he'd inflamed masses of educated young people during the long war just discontinued, and now claims the credit for having saved thousands of lives by visiting the enemy and encouraging our college boys to emigrate instead of serving the bad war. His wife's a movie star, married often enough before. I would prefer to vote for her brand of radical whoredom and anti-sexist sexism than his kind of Children's Crusading intellectualized breast-beating guilt and pan-middlebrow antipolitics that reeks of media bad faith. In your mind's eye she's always present naked and seductive. You know it's an unreachable imago; but it's her exploitation of her lithe body in the moving picture memory that makes her vociferous moral protestation against our military machine fascinating: she appears so vulnerable, so desirable, though she's not. She belongs to the same Establishment we all belong to. Free, rich, almost inspiring. But she wasn't going to show up at the cocktail party, so I'm attending out of obligation to my neighbors, who are colleagues of mine.

My wife was not in the mood however. She was watching television instead. As I passed from our bedroom through the livingroom and diningroom to the kitchen, tying my tie, buttoning my jacket, and stanching a bad razor cut on my lip, the racket of the six o'clock news was deafening. A vast defeat in the Middle East is in progress: cities are being ripped apart by a dozen small armies of ideological bandits, and tanks and armored cars are machinegunning the populace in the streets, cannonading hospitals and hotels, schools and office buildings and apartment houses, all in full color. There are earthquakes in the Alps, assassinations in four capitals; tens of thousands of men and women are parading with banners against three governments. In the Far East, the jungles are being put to the torch, and somewhere a million peasants and urban families are being marched into the swamps by teenaged troops to perish. She sits there at the kitchen table watching intently, as though it concerns us. She says out loud, "In the Southern Hemisphere, on two continents, there have been thirteen coups d'etats this past week alone. Guerrillas are proclaiming victory in twenty-one different countries." The kitchen is quiet, the canary is singing in concert with the explosions emanating from the television set.

On the table, beside her elbow, is our little son, naked, propped up in the plastic seat, his six months' old head waggling like a rubber doll's, chubby arms flapping spastically and his legs kicking, their tender toes spread wide. Can he see what's occurring on the television screen? He seems excited by it, his eyes and mouth are working silently, his tongue pushing out ribbons of liquid and lumpy cheese in little dribbles as the explosions of rockets flare out before him. She seems bemused by the vistas of terror through the billowing smoke and flame. I think myself that the infant is too near the edge of the table; but I stand there in the door behind her, tying my tie again and watching the screen. She puts her cigarette in the saucer of her coffee cup, sets it down and reaches over to switch channels. I want to warn her not to let the infant sit there unguarded, when she hesitates, glances at him, puts her left hand out as if to touch his chest, and leans far over in her chair to reach for the knob. At that instant, the baby lurches up and tips forward, and falls—plop! like an inanimate doll, like a heavy and waterfilled rubber doll—face forward, between her outspread legs, to the floor. The thud is awful. Silence. It doesn't move. She sits up, a soundless cry issuing from her opening mouth, her eyes dilated with horror, as though she is a peasant woman in a rice paddy seeing her child murdered before her face.

I stand frozen, my hands at my throat holding the ends of my tie. I feel her anger at the TV, and at herself: it is flaring out from behind the mask of her face. Then I step forward swiftly, stoop for the little creature, thinking that if it were only stunned I could give it mouth-to-mouth resuscitation. Perhaps its own softness meant it wouldn't be damaged despite the dead fall from the table top. It's all sheer carelessness, I think, and neglect of the simple rules of conduct. This infant boy, if it lived, will grow up damaged and return to haunt us, a threat somehow. I hope it won't but I know it will somehow.

As I cradle him in my arms, my wife wakes from her vision of frozen horror, her rage bursts from her, and she kicks the television set over on its face. A flash of fire comes from it as it short-circuits, and acrid smoke bursts up at us. Glass from the exploding vacuum tube and the screen flies everywhere in fine needles. She utters a scream that rises piercing, and becomes a long wailing that is choked off by a breathless sob.

KASSANDRA

In TEN YEARS, you'll forgive this night."

Never.

"Another ten, and you'll forget it."

Never.

"Ten more, and you'll wonder what the fuss was about."

Never, I said, finally.

Cocksure. But it went beyond that with him. Decathlon Silver Medallist. I'd watched him scoring all those years at school. He knew it, too. And after a triumphal return from the Games, he came to me at Thanksgiving. I was alone in our Newport place, Mother and Father away at St. Moritz, my future husband grounded in San Francisco. Years of adoration—now there he stood at the door, the very form my eyes had admired in action on the fields. My knees quailed. Who wouldn't have let him in, and be glad to. We made drinks and talked, gazing out into the gray, deserted lagoon, where hundreds of shrouded boats rocked their masts in unison, swayed by the pelting of the season's first storm.

Though fame had just come to him, his reputation was

really long-established with me: my Sisters had each taken him on, and boasted of it. Charming, all muscle, and rare skill—who wouldn't have. Yet I'd held out. Still here he was, as if he were keeping a card on our Class in my Sorority, all of us scattered around the world now a year after graduation. For five years I'd eluded him. It was the only promise my mother ever exacted from me: not him. Not that I possessed the strength to keep that vow. Twice luck was with me because of the ways things fell out. The first time, Dad's plane to Los Angeles was scratched, and he stayed on in Palo Alto to take me to dinner. The next time my turn came round to be initiated into the mysteries, Mom's mother died in her sleep, and I took flight for Syracuse. Close calls.

Two martinis towards the evening, another front of the storm pouring black, heavy clouds in low from the wild Pacific everywhere to the west, the fireplace burning mossy oak logs. The Silver Medallist lies glowing at ease on our thick buffalo robe, the orange light glancing warmly over the harsh facets of his unmarked face. No escape this time. My belly seems as hot as the flames pouring up into the chimney. Between my legs a giant rose opens slowly, its petals twisting, rustling almost audibly. An hour and more I hold out, until the docks and the boats vanish, drowned in the dark and pounding rain. I don't want him, though that rose sighs. I keep him off, making him tell me about the Games. No use. He simply stands and removes his clothes. After which it is nothing for him to strip me naked. Yet, in some infinitely small place somewhere behind my forehead my whole, true self is compressed, concealed from him. Before I slip, frenzied, into the net of his arms and am grasped by his wall-hard thighs, I am capable of one thing: I take my grandmother's diamond from my throat. I can recall that I managed to unfasten that tight antique catch on the fine platinum chain, despite my trembling fingers. And that I placed it on the night table beside my parents' bed.

Nevertheless I fought him all night. What it was really like, I cannot say. Not since then, certainly not before then, have I experienced such a long, dark night. Rape we call it nowadays. Perhaps it has always been rape. Yet to be truthful, I wasn't violated. Passion, and possession too. Not union. We entered it consciously, and, after a short sleep as profound as coma, emerged at dawn fully conscious again. Knowing him, rather knowing his track record, how could I have been surprised. Or blamed myself. We become utterly our bodies in such hours. All right. But it may also happen that we are outside them at the same time, watching. You read of people who die, and say they have looked down at themselves and said farewell—only to return, to be called back or forced once more into the partnership through the intervention of a doctor or some passerby that found them just in time. So with me that night. Not right away. After our first bout, before the ecstasies that were to come.

Where was he? I heard my hidden self ask. He'd come for me; he was taking me; I'd taken him to me—yet I sensed that he was not there at all. Though not a machine, the selfloving stud you meet and even take on sometimes for the hell of it. Something else. I was afraid, not of his absence from me, but from himself. I could endure the not having him—almost all of us have known that agony. But not the horror of the latter. For one night, I'd thought, I would have that beauty I'd missed for five years, just as my Sisters had had. This was unimaginable. Towards morning, hatred—its metallic taste filled my throat—turned what the sweet, rich flesh gave to sudden harshness. And even then, not to the lips and tongue: but towards the one who woke and watched us; my self in me. All through the dawn, through the hour of dropping silence between two waves of the vast storm that kept on coming in wet masses from the tumbling skies, lit at last by a cold light in the gray east from a sun that would not be seen for three more days.

What was it? I wondered. What was so terribly wrong? I was too young then to know. And he was aware of it; he knew. It made him cruel. I had come to, raw, weeping. I didn't know that it was despair, that I had been destroyed somehow forever. After twenty years, I know what a night like that should end like—not with uncontrollable weeping and a body that is one, great, torn wound. Quite the opposite, in fact: a body that may seem to be crushed, powerless to move, but nonetheless a body that smiles, humming with quiet praise as it knits itself miraculously again, and rises as though just created like beauty itself from the spume of the black waves rolling against the shore. No, it was not like that. And he knew it. He was cruel, never drying my tears, never consoling me for what he'd done to me. Unlike the others, I'd guessed his secret: all the gifts were his but one. He had no...what? No soul. His prowess, his fine form, his irresistible charm—it was monstrous. He knew I'd glimpsed that emptiness even before we sank through midnight. Yet I'd gone on with him, knowing what I did, until morning. Out of what necessity, because I was too young to know better? Perhaps. Now I guess that it was compassion. That, or perhaps unable to believe that such a thing can be, needing to hope that it might not be. Or, miserable that I could have been so deluded, mistaken in my longing, in my body's response to him.

He was cruel because he could be nothing else. Perhaps he wanted to disclose that secret to me, as if my sharing it could lessen the burden of nullity. Had he soothed me in his

arms, had he pretended that all was well with us, that our
night of hard loving was something to be remembered as
one of the possible fulfillments of life, the sort of thing that
comes into existence, and remains, he'd have been kinder
than most men. Though I should have hated myself for
letting him pretend. Instead, he showed me truth—and it
was too cruel to be borne. Adding those hateful words,
"You'll forgive," and, "You'll forget...."

And as I swore, I've never forgiven, nor forgotten what
I suffered that night. Rape's such a weak word for it. A
thing without a soul in my arms. A thing like that in me.

When he left, he took something from me. Not what
he'd come for—although there have been moments when I
was nearly ready to give it to a lover. He took my
grandmother's diamond pendant. He didn't think I'd seen
him pocket it while he dressed, as I lay on my parents' bed,
tearblinded, my legs and arms strengthless. As he went
out, he said, "At least you'll never have to see me again, if
that's how you feel."

I'll see you dead first! I choked out.

Down the hall, laughter. Laughter as the door blew in
under a gust, and was yanked shut once more. Outside,
laughter through the cold sheets of rain, the sloshing of his
deck shoes on the wooden planks as he trotted away.

I couldn't know how much I'd meant what I'd said in
my rage that morning. After twenty years I realize it,
neither having forgiven, nor hardly forgotten that night.
Now he lies here before me in the Hyacinth Viewing Room.
He did well in life for twenty years. He made a fortune in
yacht brokerage right here in Newport, more than ten
million a year in sales. He couldn't have missed. Today
there's not a foot of dockage to be had for money or love.
And I am down here by mischance, clearing up the estate
after the fire, only to see the obituary. He died by water.

Aboard some plutocrat's 220-foot cruiser, the Palace, that runs aground in a fog off Anacapa and breaks up in the darkness. He was found drifting in his lifejacket two days later, miles and miles away. And he looks marvelous: the soft blonde hair silvery after twenty years, the squares of the bronzed face hardly needing the cosmetician's brush. Dressed appropriately: the sportsman's blue blazer, the white flannels, the graceful black patent leather slipons. Calmly sleeping at ten in the morning. Viewing's set for eleven. I'm quite alone with him in this airconditioned chamber heaped with floral arrangements: anchors, cruisers, sailboats. The ventilators purr; the lights are very low; the electric candles flicker beside the bier.

When the sad Muzak comes on, I realize it's late, almost time for the obsequies. Nothing is changed; nothing is solved; nothing more is to be known. It comes to me then, like an inspiration: my jewel's with him still! I want it back. Against the force of my loathing, I reach over into his coffin—oh, it's fine polished rosewood, with heavy antique bronze moldings for handles—and put my hands to his neck. Yes, beneath the knot of the crimson and white silk rep, there's a lump. My fingers thrust through the shirt— my eyes, I realize, are shut tight against the vision of that immobile carcass full of cold, blue chemical fluids—and they yank. The big, oval gem, with its large, oldfashioned facets, comes away in them with a bit of chain, not the fine platinum of my grandmother's legacy but some contemporary 18-karat goldwork in flat, S-shaped links. The Muzak turns up: his family and friends will be filing in any minute now.

I have to get away. Through the Exit on the other side of that coffin. The door's flush in the wall, without a knob. How does it work? Behind the recessed panels around the ceiling, the lights are brightening. A plate beside the door has two switches in it—which one's for what? I flick one. The door doesn't budge. But there's the sound of machinery somewhere near me. Turning, I see a panel in the far wall slide away, and then, the whoompf! of a gas furnace igniting beyond it. A sudden whoosh, with a flare of intense fires. Whirring of belts. The far end of the coffin drops away, and his body begins sliding out, as though on some plank, head first through that opening in the wall. The feet tilt up in their shiny black shoes, and he slides helplessly, steadily down towards the flames. As the feet disappear, another panel with a thick, quartz glass window comes down, sealing the chute. The whole room flickers as the body seethes in the blast of that incinerator. Now the top panel of the coffin is swung up again, and the empty box remains here with me, its satiny white padding molded in the shape of his missing form. I don't know whether I'm laughing or crying; but I fumble at the other switch. The door slides away noiselessly before me, and I step through and down the narrow corridor as fast as I can, my heels turning in the thick, brown carpeting.

At the other end, the heavy door yields easily, and I find myself out on the black asphalt of the parking lot, dazzled by the August sun overhead. Lincolns, Cadillacs, Mercedes, and a notable number of Rolls Royces are moving sedately in line towards the entrance of the mortuary and chapel: many are coming to pay their respects. Getting into my car, I drop my grandmother's diamond into my change-purse. My hands are shaking, and it takes a little time for me to get my key into the ignition. I can hardly see through my sunglasses. But I drive out as fast as I dare, trying not to think of the fuss that is being made back there behind me now.

ESAU

I'D BEEN TOLD to keep out of Nazareth. Or if I visited, not to stay the night. Nothing good ever comes out of Nazareth, runs the saying in Israel. Or if I stayed the night, not to set foot in Shechem: there would only be trouble.

Well, I stayed in Nazareth. In the last decade it's been built over in Wonderland style, with special viewing spots in the religious compounds, great openings in the floors so that you can stare down into the underground warrens, the cave doors and foundations of the ancient little stone houses. All above ground is new stone, Italian-designed, slick and solid kitsch. Arranged to facilitate people-moving, as the saying runs among the aerospace architects who construct our Disneylands. I stayed in Nazareth, ate lamb kebab, drank the raw 777 brandy, and slept poorly. The next morning, right in that vast and vacuous cathedral built over Mary's Well, I ran into my own brother, whom I hadn't seen in twenty years, and his sister.

It was a surprise. Slight shock too. He didn't look well. His great bony frame wasn't clothed in fine muscle as once it had been in the days of our youth. He'd shaved that woolly russet beard, and lost most of his thatch of dark-red

105

hair: liverish tufts stuck out over his ears and hung down in hanks over the soiled color of his check shirt. And he obviously hadn't shaved for a week: the scraggly stubble was a patchwork of white and tobacco-yellow, redblack and gray. He was nervous-looking, his hands trembled, those formerly rocklike hands. And the way she behaved with him, she might have been his wife. I had never met her before. She'd been born to some father or other after he'd been carried off to Israel by our mother, when the marriage broke apart. He'd visited us a few times, finished work on his degree, and dropped from sight. I'd been busy with my own life, which was unstable as it was, moving here and there every year or so, getting settled only to have to uproot us all and move on again as opportunities called.

"Come stay with us," she said, resting her hand on my arm. Hot little fingers, and moist. She was tanned, or very dark; her hair thick, black and worn long like a girl's; her breasts high and hard. She wore her jeans tight; her lavender chiffon blouse was rolled and tied in a knot over her midriff. Full of silver jewelry she was: bracelets, anklets, rings; necklaces of old ivory, amber and topaz on gold chains draped her neck and swung heavily on those fine breasts. She was a woman with whom you were promptly a friend, and soon a lover ... if she wished to take you. Her voice was hoarse, low, guttural. Well ... I said.

"Don't be foolish. You're coming to us, and that's that!" my brother growled. "We have no time for manners."

They lived near Shechem, a field away from the hilltop, the ancient place up there. It was quite illegal, he said, and he didn't give a damn. Let them come and try to evict them. His writing was more important—he had to be at the source. So far, there had been letters, warnings, and threats. But this morning the notice had come from

Jerusalem, REGISTERED and SPECIAL DELIVERY, handed
through the door by a smirking Nazarene lad on a donkey,
who'd had the impudence to tweak her nipple as he passed
her at the gate. "Things are coming to a pass," he said. How
much longer he could hold out against the local population
of Druzes and Muslims, and the Jewish State as well, he
didn't know. But I could help. How could I? I said. "You'll
see when you're home with us," he said mysteriously. She
laughed.

As we drove over goat tracks in the jeep, the air grew
very still. The morning sun was blazing near the zenith;
the sky had retreated to infinity, and the earth seemed to
heave up solid tides of heat. The *chamsin* wind that had
blown in from the high desert to the east for two days now
had suddenly stopped, and the land sizzled in blinding
silence beneath the heavy pressure of that mass of unmoving air.

The path wreathed about the base of the high hill of
Shechem. We turned off due east of it, about 7 km. from the
highway running north-south on the west, and bisecting
the Galilee. On a low mound his house squatted, a shack of
white stucco, three boxes around an ancient olive. Down
the slopes to the east were groves of olive trees. Out front
there was a rickety bench, some geraniums in pots of hard
clay, some cactus along the walls, and a swinging wooden
gate tacked together from old shipping crate planks. A
miserable pair of date palms shaded the front door.

We skidded up, his sister and I hopped out, and he
parked the jeep round the back. We went inside and sat
under the olive tree with beers. It might have been Arizona
or New Mexico, a shack like that, the kind you see on the
back roads in the desert, abandoned years ago.

He was very nervous. Three longhandled spades
leaned against the wall. He pointed at them. "We're going

to work now. They're coming at sundown to get us out, if I know those *chaverim!*" What kind of work? I wondered. "You'll see, my fine, smoothie brother." He spat into his palms and rubbed them. His sister came and sat next to me on the old collapsed divan, put her arm round my neck and squeezed me, laughing, "We are all together in this now." In what? I wondered. "Just wait," he gloated, "there's only one way to win, and it's starting now. Listen!"

I listened. Out of the silence out there I could hear the change in things. I could feel it in my prickling skin. My hair seemed to erect itself, each strand separating, rising and tingling. The atmosphere seemed to grow denser yet, darker and hotter, if that was possible. What's happening? I asked. "The sandstorm's coming." What? I didn't believe him. They took me by my arms and led me outside. They pointed to the east. Sure enough, the horizon had changed: a great yellow-gray cloud loomed from the very earth, from the hills beyond the Jordan; it billowed into the sky.

"It's coming!" they both shouted at once in my ears. And she bit my ear, rubbing her breast against my right arm. He stood pointing at that cloud. She put her hot little hand under my belt as I stared at that incredible horizon, that smoky cloud that was all whirling sand, not vapor. Her hand thrust down behind me, wriggled down to my buttocks: her finger pressed into the cleft and scratched. She was playing. "Now, now," she muttered in that low vibrating voice, and patted me in front. "Let's not get excited—there's work to be done." My knees were watery as I followed them into the house, where we locked the windows, and sat for a supper of olives, bread and cheese.

Then, as we crouched at the low wooden table, finishing our sweet mint tea, the storm struck the house and went over with a terrific roar, the sand drumming on the tin roof, the sound of pouring rain. For an hour we didn't move, but sat on that sunken old divan, smoking and waiting in the dimness of the early dusk, inside that dark storm of sand, waiting for the night to come.

When it faded out, my brother jumped up and handed us the spades. "Let's work before they come for us!" We stepped out the front door, rather climbed up into it, for the sand was heaped about the house clear to the tops of the windows, and we had to scrabble up and pull our bodies through. I thought we were going to try to clear it away from the windows, but I was wrong. "There's only one way to keep the house from filling up with sand," he said, "and that's to close it up ourselves." It puzzled me, but I accepted his logic: after all, it's his country; he should know what he's doing.

For an hour we worked madly, shoveling sand from the heaps that lay everywhere outside now: fine, golden desert sand scintillant with sharp white crystals. We covered over the windows completely, up to the roof. "Now, when the storm returns in an hour, nothing will get into the house. We're safe: it's sand against sand!" He laughed.

Then we could hear motors gunning up from down below, sirens crying, and we saw the lights flashing red from all sides. "The soldiers have us surrounded," he yelled, "but they'll never get in, and they'll never get us out of here now!" At that moment, the storm swept back over us from the other side of the house with a tremendous, biting blast. We slid back in through the top of the door, and set to shoveling and shoring the sand up from inside. We could hear the furious shouts of the officers and the troopers calling outside in that howling, burning, dry hurricane of sand. We almost pitied them out there, standing up under it and trying to scrape the sand away from the windows and doors, if they could find them. It was blowing back and covering us over as fast as they could shovel it away.

"You see?" she said, "he's right. It's sand against sand." Now it was still inside, the air soft and quiet as a tomb. We sat down, all three together, on that broken old divan to wait for the morning. I put my arms about them both. Their heads lay on my shoulders, and they slept like children on a long journey. I remember the candle on the table guttering out.

JACOB

On THE MORNING of my fortieth birthday, we woke in London. Back home it was Thanksgiving Day, just as on the day I was born. It's no holiday in England though. Sitting over strong tea and damp toast in Durrant's Hotel in Mayfair, my wife said that she would buy me a present—I had only to name something I'd always wanted. A houndstooth sportcoat, I said. That was what occurred to me as she spoke. She smiled. "Then a houndstooth jacket it will be!"

Off to Regent Street. Cold, raining, a dreary day, just as it usually is on my birthday. Into Austin Leeds, Ltd. Up, up to the third floor. The salesman is tall and elegant in his proper pinstripe suit of black. Long ashblonde hair, ruddy cheeks with a network of fine crimson whiskey tracings on his nose. He knows just what I need, and leads us to a quiet corner. My wife seats herself on a comfortable leather pouf, crosses her legs splotched with oily spots from the messy weather, and lights one of her oval Turkish cigarettes. I stand waiting before the triptych mirror. He brings out a beautiful jacket, trim in its detailing and cut perfectly. It is a subtle green, like young grass, hatched with silver houndstooth checks. It is a fine cashmere tweed, light, shapely, lined with red and gold silk paisley. It fits me as perfectly as if it had been bespoke for me alone.

And yet, it feels not right somehow. She sits smoking, patiently observing me as I turn about in the mirrors, and she smiles with pleasure. But I find I am growing angry. "What's wrong?" she asks sympathetically, kindly, concerned. Perhaps she's thinking I am not going to accept this gift from her after all. At last I realize what troubles me. I had been feeling the heavy weight of the shoulders: it is padded. I mention this to the salesman. I ask if the tailors will remove these lumps. I can sense that if I cannot carry them now in the fitting, I certainly shall not bear them when I return home.

"But my dear fellow, this is the way it's styled, you see?" he says with what seems to me a mellow condescension. Take them out, I say. "We call them angel's wings," he adds, "and we cannot remove them from your garment." Well, you must. Do it for me, I plead with him: they won't do in America. "Quite out of the question," says he, sneering at me now. "I can't change the correct style only to suit you, and I won't have that splendid coat altered to suit you either. It's one of a kind, so far as I am concerned."

But the weight of these wings will oppress me at home, I say. I find that I am also somewhat worried about the extravagant price of this jacket too, but I say nothing to her about it. Instead, I say, I am buying it, and I'll have to wear it, so it ought to be done as I wish it.

The man is silent. "It's you must choose," he says finally. "Well?" my wife chimes in. "Take it or leave it," he announces, his teeth showing in a harsh grin, not at me, but to my form in the mirror. My wife sighs deeply.

It is already darkening outside, and the evening rush hour has started on Regent Street. It is very chilly and wet: weather that cuts like an ax into the bone.

SAUL OF TARSUS

W<small>E ARE A SMART BUNCH</small> of moneymakers out here. Rolling country, small hills, lakey dales, winding pikes and historical roadhouses that saw Revolutionary battalions tramping and camping. Somewhat more than ninety minutes from the Street, it's a commute; but worth it to have golf and tennis for the wife, a barn and horses, some sheep and goats for the kids, a thirteen-room ranch house with remote control stereo laid on in each one, including the laundry. As for donations, per capita we give equal to Beverly Hills, and they are showoffs. Among our notables we've got some smart, ex-Yeshiva *chaverim* who can read your Torah forth and back again while figuring fortunes in silver, corn, soybeans, eggs, and pork bellies. Don't ask what we need. Here we do all the asking. And answering.

But it was the Ladies Auxiliary that heard about this *wunderrebbe* and made the offer to get him out for the High Holidays. Could he sing, they said. Not even a Jan Peerce could sing like he could sing, they said. In three days they pooled ten thou. A trifle. Sent off a cashier's check months in advance, on Passover, in fact, as demanded by his agency, and talked of nothing else for six months. When he came, we would all hear something. As though a Messiah was going to stop by.

They picked him up early Friday morning at the station near the Pennsylvania border, outside New Hope. Showed him off at their annual Founders and Donors Luncheon. A plump and glowing son of a bitch, was what I thought: not a shiny patch on his fine serge of midnight blue—banker's stripes; silk vest, oyster-toned; textured silk shirt; a ruby cabuchon stickpin popping out of his gray tie, also of a silk woven heavy enough to be tapestry; a fawn-gray homburg; and Bally boots of satiny calfskin as fine as his silk socks. Pinky rings: one diamond set in white gold, surrounded by rubies, the other a star sapphire the size of a robin's egg. A golden goatee, and thick golden eyebrows over black and Byzantine eyes. It he weren't a cantor, well then he had to be the bagman out of Vegas. There goes that ten thou—with Rosh Hashonah and Yom Kippur into the bargain. Go trust our Sisterhood, women who live on rep and rumor. Yet, I must admit, so do we in the Market.

Friday evening. Town empty and Temple packed. The hard core is our Seventy Families. Such great expectations for this New Year's. Sitting among these folk, well fed, handsomely groomed, and dressed with overflowing stylishness, was in itself exciting. But the richness of their mingled scents was intoxication. The throaty, spicy odor welled up radiating from the women in the warming air of the Temple: its dark muskiness palpitated from them until your head floated from your shoulders, adrift on waves of fat, animal incense. Their vitality heated us all, and their glowing skins swelled moist, supporting their heavy necklaces and bracelets, and making a faint tinkling sound as they swayed in their seats. These splendid women of the Seventy: these wives and daughters with fine torsos like

ripe fruit in the finest of cashmere and sheer camel wool:
their glistening coiffures, from black to flossy platinum:
they were an autumn garden among us, and all our wealth
seemed to emanate from the darkness between their full
and weighty thighs.

Their marvelous Reb Saul has mounted the stage.
Behind him, the satin-gowned singers are choiring. He has
a fine voice. But, compared to Peerce or Tucker this is no
cantor at all. Why should anyone notice, though? Their
money is singing in their skulls.

For our sermon his text is, "Hear, O Israel." In a
brightedged *heldentenor* pealing, he calls "Hear, O Israel!"
And stops. The quiet grows until the indrawn breath of our
thrilled matrons can be heard sighing out once more. At the
rostrum, before the altar, standing in the purpleshadowed
vibrant spotlight, he shimmers in his midnight blue robe.
The white shawl over his shoulders plays cold, blue flame
as his stocky chest rises and falls. Diamond and sapphire
sparks flash at us from his pudgy fingers. Everyone waits
for him to speak. At last he does. "Do you know what I shall
now say?" And the women and the men of the Seventy
Families, ranked in the costliest pews before him, cry out,
involuntarily, "Yes, yes." "Good! Then I don't have to
speak any further!" Briskly, he turns and strides from the
dais, and vanishes in the wings.

A long silence in the Temple. The entire congregation
is dumb. Our rabbi scurries forward to close the service,
his hands fluttering as he intones, "And thou shalt love the
Lord thy God with all thy heart, and with all thy soul, and
with all thy might." We all know that line. "Omayn," the
crowd responds in mutters as it rises, disappointed, and
starts filing out as to a funeral. No one says anything.
Outside, there is the sound of the doors of Cadillacs,
Mercedes, and Lincolns slamming, motors firing up and

the swishing of heavy whitewalled tires as they pull away.

What transpired that night at our rabbi's, I don't know. But the service on the next evening begins again in the same manner, as though nothing unusual had occurred. The Sabbath is being closed, the first Sabbath of our New Year. Everything is as it was the preceding day. Once again, the choir choiring, and our guest, the *wunder-rebbe* Saul, letting loose that tenor in a rather impressive cantilena, something it seems to me this time that sounds like another ten thou. His round face glistens with the effort, his throat swells mightily, yet his eyes, seen from the last row where I sit, are not caught in that passionate ululation—they are fixed on me, on my forehead, or fixed through me. Frankly, I have not shut mine in prayer nor cast them on the book in prayer: hence I can observe him, even though he never sees me: his focal point is deep inside the back of my head. Which is nowhere, really, neither here nor there.

Tonight his text is, "The Horn." Once more he cries out, "Our God, and God of our Fathers!" And stops. And waits, just as he waited yesterday. Everyone waits with him. I notice that our rabbi, and the seven who advise him, the Rolls Royce gang we call them, are glancing at one another, faint smiles struggling free at the corners of their mouths. They are going to put him in his place. There must have been telephone conferences this morning, Sabbath or no Sabbath. Our glittering guest smiles too, and then coos to us all, "Does everybody know what I shall say now?" The seven headmen, these chiefs among our Seventy Families, rumble challengingly, "No, no!" Reb Saul clasps his *tallith*, looking as though he's hanging on his own prayer shawl for support, his polished toes an inch or so above the floor of the stage, lifts his eyes to the candelabrum over our heads, whirls about once to survey the Ark behind the altar, and shrugs, speaking not to us but to the emptiness of the Temple ceiling. Simply, truthfully, he says, "If you don't know, then how can I ever explain it to you?" Then, as briskly as the evening before, he skips into the wings.

The departure of the congregation takes place anew. Only this time it's faster: there is frustration and rage indoors, and a loud, unholy buzzing outside. Limousine doors are wrenched open and violently shut all over the parking lot, and cars tear away with tires squealing. It is miraculous that no one's knocked down and killed within the Temple grounds.

To my surprise we are not, however, done with the fellow. Had I been consulted by our wisemen, I should have advised them to swallow it and forget the whole affair. This trickster may be a holy guy of some kind, but he is more than a match for our brokers of pelf and power. But I was not consulted. In our community, wisdom is measured, as elsewhere, by those who own most of everything. The rest take our tips from them. Though there are few enough crumbs strewn about the high seats: they lick their plates clean, in fact.

So that here we are at last a week later at the Day of Atonement. All our beauties have fasted: yet they glow more than ever like the sleek and fullbodied kine they are. Hunger has flushed their cheeks and touched up their eyes with light. Many have come and gone out of the Temple all day for Kaddish services: we all have our dead, even the rich. And we have our *wunderrebbe* back again, lo! for the closing service on this Sabbath afternoon. Judging by the serious mien on the faces of our leaders and rabbi, real business is in order. We gather that there is actually a double-or-nothing bet laid down—the service and sermon will go through as it should, or he shall refund everything,

tonight's fee and the first twenty thousand bucks. We are
at the bottom line. It is his single wit against the collective
smarts of the seven of the Seventy.

The day is our most solemn. The autumn weather has
been filled with glory: dry, bright, colorful: Indian summer
commencing here in Indian Hills.

And his voice is glorious too. The famished choir
chants from the pits of their empty bellies. A Kol Nidre to
end all Kol Nidres. Truly, Reb Saul has a rare voice! In it we
hear not merely the chant of ages, but the chanting of
Israel's sorrows, twenty-five hundred years of sorrow.
Such a song must make good all the vows made to Him,
vows unfullfilled and unfullfillable. It will make good
moreover the ghosts of promises made but not kept since
Moses smashed the Tablets against the Golden Calf at
Sinai. When the *wunderrebbe* finishes singing, everyone in
the Temple weeps, even our tough leaders whose eyes had
not moistened even at the funerals of their fathers and
mothers. Oh, he is a pro!

And the text? Surely, a thirty thousand-dollar text:
"The Lord our God, The Lord is One." For the third and
last time he intones, halfcrooning, halfpleading, "On this
day of fasting, I beg Him to pardon my sins. May he answer
me! May He say, I have forgiven!" And he stops. The
bosoms of the wives and daughters rise and fall, making
the light itself tremble. Down in their front rows sit our
leaders, waiting him out, confident they have won. He is
confident too. His hands lift, palms up. He gazes down at
them. Finally he says, "Do you know what I am going to
say to you this evening?" Half our congregation, by
prearrangement, nod "Yes, yes!" and the other half shake
their heads firmly "No, no!" Reb Saul beams at all of us. His
bejeweled fingers grip his silk shawl, flaring white, pink,
blue darts of flame into our eyes.

"Excellent!" he says in that clarion voice. "Your troubles are over. Those who understand will now explain it to those who don't!" Before anyone can react, he skips to the altar, reaches up and closes the Ark, spins around thrice on tiptoe, raises the shofar to his lips and blows a mighty blast that pins everyone into their seats.

The High Holidays are ended. The New Year has begun. No one's moved. A silence devastating. Then, an inarticulate murmuring, the susurration that comes from inside a nest of hornets, hums through the Temple. But louder than that, from outside, sounds the brilliant burr and gargling roar of the exhaust pipes of the Ferrari that ignites, shifts swiftly through the first and second gears and into third, accelerating now into the night, heading towards New Hope and the setting sun.

MOSES

FROM THANKSGIVING ON, another winter of ice-age snows. With the solstice a cold wave moves in over the entire region: by day the skies are white and void. The bleached sun rolling low in the south and glancing off the endless billowing drifts never lifts the temperature above zero: the thinned air hisses and shimmers all night with the utter transparency of 20-below. The constellations are packed with so many more stars that had never been guessed at before: they are sharp as needles, and their faint blue radiance floats back from the vast, endless mantled earth. Then for a week in January the auroras spread their filmy veils flowing between us and the heavens, pulsing with cold and brilliant ineffable hues. At midnight the stillness is broken by the ripping groans of trees splitting here and there through the woods and orchards. Nightlong the owls hoot, mating calls floating now near, now echoing far off invisibly. The crust of ice forming roughly on the snow is covered every day or so by a new powdery fall of crystals materializing out of the empty air and whirling off in dazzling coruscations all afternoon, keeping the paralyzed world freshly swept with whiteness, layer laid upon layer again. The fences have sunk from sight, and all the fields

and pastures merge into one expanse. A few cardinals light
our feeding tray with bursts of crimson; the bluejays crash
savagely down, scattering poor and ragged sparrows; the
waxwings pluck vainly at ice-glazed berries.

Two hundred years ago there had been longhouses in
our orchard. All winter long Senecas or Oneidas lay
wrapped in pelts, pots of squirrel or dogmeat stew simmer-
ing on the embers of hearths down the lengths of their one
great room where two dozen or more families endured such
freezes. It is so cold now there are not even rabbit tracks to
be seen. Too cold to ski, too biting to snowshoe or toboggan.
We pass in muffled silence along these walled paths plowed
for us between the buildings. We drink far too much on the
weekends. Heavy icicles fringe the eves, some a yard long.
And the frost persists, week after week. In February a
week's moist and warm air flows in from the sea two
hundred miles to the southeast, bringing a sickening slump
with it. Midwinter thaw. Underneath the white world
things seem to shift about as though the frozen ground
heaved, turning and slowly swelling and reshaping itself
before our eyes. Then other waves of storms come in,
blizzards from the Lakes to the northwest burying us again
in drifts six to twenty feet high. In late March, finally,
when everyone is down, bitter and miserable with cabin-
fever—and even old, true friendships taste the dregs at the
bottom of our exhausted being—there are moist breezes
from the south and southwest, with sleeting rains slushing
the bottomless snowpack. For days icicles begin to drip and
run like faucets, then crash down dangerously. Crows sit
ranting from the empty tops of the oaks. The sun vanishes
altogether, hidden behind low, tumbling black clouds that
roll endlessly over, pouring sheets of cold water down,
torrents running over the rotting fields and broken roads
until the clay shows through at last, red mud sliding from

the banks and slashes everywhere.

It is over. People are coughing, their shadow-rimmed eyes watery with fever and bronchitis. The old among us stand up better—after seventy-five years in this hard country they are immune to all but time. Their minds hold out too; only their brains seem to decay, to rot out like the trunks fallen in our woods. Yet even this hateful sort of spring is precious to them. To them only, perhaps. We wait, saying nothing. What good after all can come of this cycle of death and rebirth each year. The soul is not nourished by seasons.

We had heard nothing from Liz and Leo since last summer. There was a card with a Mexican stamp on it. It had taken months to wander up to us here in Arcady, just below the foothills of the Adirondack Mountains. A garishly-inked blur of the usual empty beach fringed by swaying fan palms, a striped umbrella in the background, and a coffee-tanned Azteca in a string bikini who stood once, grinning ferociously, at the edge of the sand, her arms held out with longing to the flat, coppergreen lagoon. Such winters separate old friends like fossil strata in which a couple of centimeters of sandstone suggest the passage of a million years and more. Yet the past is always present, locked up in the dead record below us. And even to the living, what is time? Another thin deposit between us now, like this fading winter. Liz and Leo—what were they doing so far away there on that blank western coast of Mexico? Hadn't they been journeying to Seattle for the summer? Had the rain been too much for them? And were they still there, slung in hempen hammocks under a thatched roof, sipping margaritas while the tepid tropical rain fell all the afternoon, or watching the kids ransack the tide's edge for crabclaws and cockles, or run screaming like macaws into the small surf?

Just at the end of April, though, the crocuses up and blooming below our windows, there comes a battered, yellow Buick wagon jouncing along our rutted driveway. The maples are sprouting small green leaves, all alight, a milky furze that dresses their mossed gray limbs. The willow on the lawn is newly-dressed, a dryad in a shining, transparent, pale green shift. The oaks are budding too. The last patches of snow are shrivelling, running over the lawn in clear trickles on the downslopes, surrounded by dinged and matted grass that shows signs of life once more. And we too are here still, blinking at the creamy sun that rides every day a shade higher, gradually filling out. We're ready for them, not because they bring us any news of the great world, but because a letter arrived the other day, declaring an outing for us all. Liz wrote it in her detached manner. It told us that, having at last reached Seattle, Leo seemed tired, complaining that he hadn't recovered from that Victoria virus. That hour after hour he'd gripped the wheel of their new International Harvester wagon, white-knuckled, chewing on the inside flap of a cheek, no longer talking to them. That he'd grown changeable, preoccupied. Then irritable and absentminded. Finally, withdrawn. No sooner lodged on the small, rented islet miles out in Puget Sound, their larder stocked, the salmon rigs readied, than he'd insisted on packing, ferrying back, and turning south, south, and south again, driving over three thousand miles as though pursuing a rainbow whose foot was planted somewhere thataways. As though a pot of gold waited in Mazatlan, that billboard paradise. The only gold was dysentery, paid out by herself and the children. Leo suffered not at all in his gut. When they were taken to the hospital for two days, Leo was lost ... it must have been a suicide. What else is 57 Quaaludes? But in the end he refused to lie down at all after having paced the beach

fourteen hours, dazed, tranquilized and also horny as hell.
He came in himself for the stomach pumping—she'd found
him at the other wing when she was discharged. Meanwhile, their Harvester wagon was dismantled right beside
their cabana. Nothing left but the logo, which Leo skimmed
off into the sea. They were permitted to fly out only after
the doctor had written a very expensive report certifying to
the authorities that it had been merely food poisoning. Not
to worry: all was well—after a round of twelve electro-
shocks and eight months of intensive therapy with a
hardheaded psychiatrist. And Liz meant hardheaded—the
guy had read nothing but textbooks all his life—he thought
everything Leo had ever thought he'd thought was a myth.
And he has a point there at that, Leo agrees. Not that he
remembers much if anything of the whole year. Otherwise
his head, ha ha, is clear. So they were driving up for an
outing, she wrote. And here indeed they are, pulling up to
the house.

"Let's see if Leo's still cracking his knuckles," my wife
remarks aside, as the door swings open and Liz heaves her
thick thighs sideways to get out. Poor man, it occurs to me:
drove all the way down to that hot sea, where Charon's
barge lay hove-to outside Mazatlan waiting, and it's passed
him by. All he will have had forever now was the midlife
crisis, that dreadful pilgrimage expunged from recollec-
tion. Liz, however, chainsmoking and hacking, will remember it to us in every detail. Yet the story will lack the
one detail one cares to hear: what it felt like to stumble, to
go over the edge: that prolonged moment's months of dying,
as things silently lifted themselves from their places and
drifted outward, removing themselves from him in all
directions. That agony unknown, one lives in the poverty
of mere ignorance. Yet one lives. There is that. They have
given him life. Life in ignorance, in exchange for the

knowledge of death. His year they can never return to him. Her letter had closed by saying that Leo was even taking an interest in things again. And here he is, extricating himself from behind the wheel as their boy and girl clomp up the porch steps to where ours are waiting for them. Leo still looks like Leo. Well, we are all changed, yet no one knows.

I know. He is a frightened man. That much I discern from our conversation late that night in front of the fireplace after the rest have gone to bed. Doc Hardhead has cured him of the illusion that whole being is possible, let alone desirable. A naive wish merely. Everything is only things. Their presences have been removed. They never were. To will is false, dreaming. Willing, we add increment to increment at best, as day is added unto day, and we a sum to be totalled never. That is how things seem to him now. Not too bad at that either. And grace? I say. Leo is short, square; his hair has gone white suddenly, a thick, short-cropped thatch. The ancient acne scars are deep pocks now. He doesn't even smile at this. "What is grace?" he returns. "You surprise me. Really." Sometimes I surprise myself, I say. And go on: It's the one thing the world cannot supply. "You surprise me," he says again. But we can ourselves supply all the rest: realism, *le tacte des choses*, even, at the end, clarity, acceptance, resignation. "Enough for me," Leo murmurs, finishing his bourbon off, "no more, please. There is no other world now." But I pour myself another measure of Wild Turkey, and, laughing, I tell him: The path to the possible lies right here at one's feet. We are always and right now too on that unmarked path. And surrounded by the presences of every thing, unrevealed and luminous as these glowing coals. Grace may descend and open our eyes. Or grace may erupt from within. "Thanks, but no thanks," Leo says, holding his empty glass upside down. "I'm going to sleep. You've had enough too, brother." Just trying it on for size, I say. No harm done? "Enough is enough. What more could you need?" Myself, Leo. "Wish I could help you," is all he says.

The next morning's clear. You never can be sure around Arcady though. We'd travelled fifty miles north by noon, climbing up into the mountains. There's a place in the National Forest I know, a campground that would be empty this time of year. I am driving; Liz is beside me; Harriet's behind me and Leo next to her; the four kids are playing poker in the back, the dog between their legs serving as the support for their board. The trip's pleasant, traffic light. I am glad to find the narrow access road into the upper valleys open. The water from the snowpack above is trickling out under the snow banked on both sides of the road, and steams up on the midday warmth. Twenty miles away from the main road, the mountains are altogether deserted. We are winding along, a little too fast for comfort as Harriet keeps reminding me with taps on the shoulder, when there is an angry beeping from behind. Liz has been rattling away with her stories about their junket across America last June, and I'd not paid attention to the rear. There'd been a glint of sun off a windshield earlier; but I had not been aware that now there was a muddy jeep tailgating us, weaving from side to side. Now its horn is beeping at us. From the look of it, there were two fishermen in green-and-brown camouflage jumpsuits—their assembled rods are clipped to the roof. They are too late to do any fishing today, I remark; and besides, most of the fish are gone up here—the rain and snow is polluted by sulfuric acid from the Midwest and the streams are dead. "Let them pass," my wife urges me. I can't, the road's too narrow and the shoulders are oozing mud: they'll have to wait. They keep on pushing me, though it should be plain this big Chrysler wagon fills the road. They'd have to wait for a turnout. And five winding miles go by, up and down, with the wide places blocked by mounds of melting snow, with them pressing just behind, not letting up with that beepbeeping. I hold steady and hog the crown in the center of this road. Too damn slow for them: I can see them mouthing obscenities in my rearview mirror.

Then it happens. There is a hairpin on a downslope, and I enter it staying close on the left, even though anyone coming down from the mountains must be invisible to me if he's going to come around that bend just now. Right there that jeep makes its move, comes roaring along passing on the right. Are they crazy? I yell. As they draw alongside, the driver's shouting and thumping his horn. These upcountry Kallikaks! I laugh. But on their side, we suddenly see the road's broken right off the side of the mountain. And these two redfaced and squintyeyed characters, halfturned round at us and shaking their beercans threateningly, never even see the jagged edge of the crevasse yawning there. The jeep just hurtles out turning end over end, and vanishes. The women gasp, but I keep on, hugging the half of the road that remains to us on the left, not even tapping my brakes.

"Goodbye, you guys," our boy calls, and the other three kids laugh, as though it's the climax of some TV chase. The curve goes sloping wickedly down into a halfmile of straightaway, where I can see a shiny slick ahead: a ripple of ice where water freezes on the asphalt in the shadow of the mountain. No choice. We hit it coasting. "My god!" my wife wails from behind me. The snowtires whir as the heavy Chrysler slides out, and to our silent horror we also find ourselves flying in slowmotion off the road.

Somehow nothing more terrible happens. The car simply tilts, nosing forward, and slithers grumping down the long wet scree of slate and granite shale blasted from the flank of the mountain when the road was cut through up there. Down, down, down. We come to a rest a thousand feet below on a soft, wide spill of gravel where a stream runs clear beside a naked stand of secondgrowth birch and alder. A calm glade, the young spring sun slanting into it still from the south through the vee between two snow-covered peaks. Just right for our picnic, I hear myself saying to everyone.

For some minutes we sit there unmoving, stunned. Then Leo opens his door and gets out. Liz lets hers swing wide, but doesn't move, halfconsciously flipping a cigarette up from the everpresent pack in her fist, bringing it to her mouth and stroking her lighter across it. My wife pushes her door open wide, lets her long legs hang out, reaching to touch the solid ground. I turn and see that she has her right arm on the shoulder of our girl behind her; but she is staring at the toe of her boot, which makes a slow and thoughtful circle over a layer of rotting brown birch leaves that covers the wet pebbles. I stay in my seat, holding the wheel hard, after having cut the ignition. Leo walks around the car, kicking the tires. Three times he circles the car, inspecting the damage. His hands are on his hips. He stops finally, looking up at the mountains vaguely. He sighs deeply, and says to no one in particular, "Now whose fault was that?" Liz must recognize some oddness in his tone, for she lays a restraining hand on my arm, leans across me heavily to look up at him, and says sharply, "You know better than to blame anyone, Leo!" Leo turns his un-focussed eyes down and says sweetly, to me, I think, and not to his wife, whose tousled head lies on my chest, "What do you think of your god now?" I respond, startling him, But I have no god. "Then where in hell are we!" Some-where, Leo. "Not good enough!" We're two hours north of Arcady, I continue, and still alive. "Not good enough!" he shouts. "Leo darling—" Liz cries.

He turns, striding away to the southwest, where the weakening sun is drifting towards the shoulders of the mountains we entered an hour or so ago. The shade that lengthens over this gorge into which we have fallen seems to drop the temperature ten degrees: a sudden chill without a breeze. The sweat springing from my body runs icy down me inside my clothes. "Where are you headed?" Liz calls out plaintively. He halts, halfturned towards us in farewell, to observe, "We'll never get out alive." None of that! I hiss after him. I'm thinking of the children, who are just clambering out the back of the wagon after the dog, who sneezes violently and strolls over to the stream to lap at it. "Someone's got to pay for the accident, or we're done for. We need a scapegoat. And I'm it. So long." A wave of the hand, and he heads off.

Leo! I'm suddenly angry with him, seething inside with indignation. Liz shoves me violently out of my seat, and I am up and trotting after him. He turns slowly, smiling blissfully. I never do see his balled fist coming up, in fact: he has not swung, but only lifted it, his shoulder locked as his heels plant themselves, to meet my headlong rush. I am knocked sprawling, the wind out of my lungs, by the blow to my heart. And he resumes his deliberate stroll away into the wilderness. "Stop him!" Liz croaks. "Oh my god," my wife moans again. But the children are laughing at the tableau: this isn't serious. Yes it is. I get to my feet. A smooth stone, the size and shape of a goose egg, in my hand. Without consideration, I hurl it after Leo. It flies true; it catches him behind his right ear. He drops face down on the edge of the cold, purling brook. Harriet's voice from the car, bitter, "That's stopping him."

Leo's face is drained white; against the dingy basaltic sand where he lies, it's like the upturned belly of a dead fish. But a line of blood oozes from the corner of his mouth, congealing purplish on his chin. There is a tear welling in the corner of his eye, and its lid trembles faintly. A slow pulse in his throat beating stubbornly tells me he is coming to. He's alive, I call over my shoulder to the women.

Leaving Leo to them, I set out in the other direction, following the water. The four children trail after me; they insist on helping me search for the way out. The last thing I see, as we turn the bend, heading upstream into the woods, is Liz kneeling, cradling Leo's head upon her lap, and my wife dipping her blue bandana in the clear water. Our black mastiff's glad to be out of the car and running ahead, quartering the rudimentary track as though he were out for bear. Silently, the children file behind me. Save your strength! I have admonished them. "Why?" my son said, sceptical as always. For the way back. "Ah," he replied, as though he knew what he was saying, "I forgot about that." How could you? "Because you're always saying there's only one way to go—forward."

If that's what he's learned from me, I muse, during the next hour's trek over broken ground where the winter's debris has blocked the way along the noisy stream—timber, boulders, slides and snowfilled gullies, mushy soft ground covering the wide places around the little tributary freshets from above, full of melting ice and brush—if that is so, then I've taught a hard truth to children. Will they remember it, or even understand it later?

Then we stand, surprisingly, on a road that comes out of this wood, fording the brook at a natural dam made of gravel and flat stones, a rapids on our side, a pool below a falls on the other, and it leads away, still following the water, but on higher ground. To our left, the wall of mountain slopes almost vertically up to where the paved road rides its shoulder a thousand and more feet above, and fades away into a cold white mist that is already descending from the peak. This road's a two-wheel track, perhaps an ancient logging way. The going's easy now, and we gladly march along. Up ahead, a bend; when we approach it, the dog's on the other side, planted squarely in the middle, his hackles bristling with alarm. He sniffs the air, his great fierce head turning this way and that, his hind legs quiver visibly. That's not like this brute.

And there's a light ahead. We keep on, the dog bringing up our rear now, reluctant. The children haven't remarked his odd behavior, but follow me humming a tuneless anthem together. The light appears to be inside a house now visible through the trees. A dark, dank place it seems as we come up to it, though rather large for these parts. Gabled with Victorian scrollwork everywhere; a high porch, the bottom of the place built up twelve feet with fieldstone, all mossy with age. The wood once painted red and white had long since faded over many decades to a blackish carmine, wide swaths of mildew everywhere, and wet rot. At the roadside a mailbox on a crumbling cedar post; gothic script: Peavy. A signboard propped against the trunk of the great hemlock that stands at the start of the sinking, overgrown flagstone walk: Peonies—Honey— Flowering Judas—For Sale. Off to one side there are indeed old hives scattered among the unkempt growth of what must have been an orchard once upon a time: the hives are tumbled about, broken, buried in leaves and trash and rotten snow.

"What a witchy place!" croons Leo's girl, and they all giggle with her. On the sagging, moldy post at the top of the twelve broken steps to the high porch there's another sign, scrawled with a brush dipped in tar: Do Not Disturb. Yet another board tacked beside the screendoor: No Trespassers. The hell with that! I say to it under my breath, and rap firmly at the lintel.

No answer. Knock again. The dog, who has kept back,

and waits below on the muddy walk, growls low and warningly. Sounds from inside. A light now edging the door on the inside, a heavily-scarred oak door, its once white-painted surface all peeling, the gray grain's whorls and waves napped, roughened by long exposure. It opens slowly, scraping along the splintery threshold. An old woman stands there, shawled with an afghan, a sagging, gray cardigan buttoned over a gray flannel shirt. A black and stained serge skirt hangs to her ankles, which are covered with boots, the loose unlaced boots of a workman. She holds a kerosene lamp to us.

Have you got a telephone? I ask her. She seems not to understand me. I say that we have been in an accident, that our car has come down from the mountain, from up there. She looks at me with anger. Doesn't she believe me? Nobody's hurt, I add—but we have got to find a way up again. Can she tell me where to go for help? Behind us the dog's barking now, barking and whining at once. "Yeh'd be Jews," she mutters then, and spits with contempt. She makes to swing the door shut. But my boot's planted there. She looks down, baffled. Then she raises her lamp to peer at us again, lifting her wrinkled, brown face to study us from under the ravelled rim of a black straw bonnet she wears perched incongruously atop her head; its fusty old satin ribbons are tied beneath her chin as if they held her loose jaw and clacking dentures together in place. She is very angry. Her head shakes with rage. But my boot stays holding the door she's pressing at. Her voice grates, "That's the way for yeh now." I turn in the direction she has pointed, and the door is slammed shut.

We march down from that rickety porch. The dog's happy to be running away again, away from that place. On the road once more, and pursuing it to the right as before, we see through the thinning trees what look like distant lights. They flicker from what seems a low valley.

Setting out briskly for them, we emerge after a few hundred yards to find ourselves on sloping ground. It's darkening, and a chilling wind sweeps up at us as we move quickly down. Is it a sunken meadowland, a floodplain ahead, or deep water? The children are flagging, so I slow our pace. We can only follow where this road leads us anyway. And in the hour we discover what was barely glimpsed from the high ground we'd left behind: the road ends, abruptly, at a black lake. In fact, the road runs right down into the waters, icestrewn waters that splash up, disturbed by the wind. The shore is littered with water-logged old trees, half-floating, half-snarled in great heaps and tangles to right and left. Impassable shores, swamp, mud, dried calamus and sumac brittle in the cold, withered, and dead.

No lights anywhere. Wherever that village was, it's utterly hidden from sight now. The dog stands silent, his tail tucked between his legs, head down to the wind. The children cluster to me. Beside the road, there is a stack of old railroad ties. I am thinking that I had been hoping for salvage like that, railroad ties to shore up the borders of a rock garden I had planned once. Here they are, free for the taking. What a fortunate fall! I say smiling. The children look up at me, puzzled. The littlest one whimpers, trying not to cry. I stoop, and take her in my arms.

COURTLY LOVE

AND SHE WROTE me a letter after she'd run away from him. To say she wanted me but couldn't have me. To say she was unlisted. To say, if you please, she needed to be by herself. Not that she desires being alone. No, she aches for me from head to toe. As an ontological proposal she puts it. To be by myself. *By* meaning "beside." *By* signifying too the cause of which she might come to seem the effect. "A white phantom is what I am now," it reads, "though between us, truetempered as ever, the sword of passion lies. My darling, you must abandon the quest, abandon all questing if you wish to find me again. You will need to hunt for me no longer then. There's nothing to be found, there is no one to seek. Then I shall be for you." Nice letter for your mistress to write. The woman thinks to liberate herself by hiding. So she had left him for good—and me, imperfect as I am. How could anything be good this way?

And it was not good. Summer had passed. Autumn brought little change. New York never cooled: the days shrank drearily in dust and gritty touches of feebly circulating air. No rain or frost, no currents of piney wind from the Adirondacks or Catskills, already frozen and gray, no sleet or hint of storm from the North Atlantic. Only a stationary mass of high pressure hot air blanketing the entire zone until it seemed as if we were to have to live floundering at the bottom of a pool of acid industrial waste and the exhaust pollutants produced by all the machines that kept us going. An emergency that had not yet been conceived and grasped as the onset of a state of disaster. Rich and poor, we were all in this together. Yet everything proceeded as usual in our mighty metropolis. How could it not?

And I too went on as usual. Each morning I rose and went off to work with all the others under that sere yellowbrown pall enveloping us. Struggle never ceases. The quality of life had altered, not its style, since we can know no other here, where the poor believe themselves richer in fact than they would be elsewhere. I did not know how I missed her. We were through with one another, but not finished. There seems to be a difference. When this occurred to me, I understood that what grew in me day by day was wrath, a charge accumulating until it filled me. Where was there place in me for my bones, my organs, my muscles and flesh? Yet there was: in the mirror this scarred body seemed whole, its clothes fitting as well as ever. Was this dense wrath unreal? I knew better. One night in late November I read her letter again. There should be a clue.

And suddenly there it was: the zipcode stamped on the envelope! Flushing Meadows, in Queens. I'd never replied to that horrible farewell statement of hers; nevertheless, I thought she would use a post office box for protection, that it would be in the station near the park that had been the site of the great New York World's Fair of my childhood, erected on top of the garbage dumps that had filled the swamps of old, making marvellous futuramas out of the midden of the present. If *I* could, anyone would find her, even he, the husband that sent her an allowance. No matter what it cost him he was satisfied to support her; he's that way; he loves her; it's all he knows. By keeping her, he kept me too; and by keeping me, he kept her. That is what she believed.

And thought would last forever. However, we changed, if she did not. Whereupon she had disappeared, upsetting the whole world. To find her again now is not so easy. I could try. If it weren't too late. Although it was past midnight, I'd never get to sleep: that numeral would dance in the darkness before me. I dressed and went out.

And it was 1:00 when I reached Flushing Meadows, in Queens. The nighttime was less suffocating than our days: the inversion had lifted and let some of the ruined atmosphere drain away. Overhead hung the rancid half of the old moon, sagging, jaundiced. The borough was quiet: Sunday night and people getting whatever rest there might be for the week to come. I found the post office: its empty flagpole stuck out over the sidewalk. She should be holed up somewhere within walking distance, and not in an apartment: she needs space to dance in. It would be some loft. Alongside the El tracks were old factory buildings, garages, warehouses. In five minutes' cruising I spotted the only light left in this sleeping world. She never sleeps. There she'd be.

And was. I ascended to the seventh floor in a freight elevator large enough to carry my car too, and knocked on the ironsheeted factory firedoor. Music inside somewhere, muffled by thick walls: her radio playing as always. No answer. I kicked at it three times. She knows my kind of banging. No answer. I am turning away for good when there is the scuffling of slippered feet. Five complex seals are unbolted, unlocked, the handle is wrenched from my hand and the heavy door heaved at me. I am stunned by the blow to my nose and forehead, and blinded by the bank of spotlights suddenly glaring right at me. Confused, rocking on my heels, I hear her singing out, "Darling, is it you?" As though she had never broken it off, had never changed utterly, never fled or left me. Which she had.

And leading me by the hand, stroking my forehead, kissing my nose and eyes tenderly, she reproached me for my silence. "I knew you'd find me—if only you looked. But, you didn't." As though I'd given up, refused, rejected or betrayed her. Which I hadn't. I'd accepted her loss, and gone on alone with nothing, certainly not myself. She was my being, wherever that is. This occurred to me as I brimmed with that fossilizing wrath that filled the soft inner parts, which were life. Love's anguish. The cloying incense of chrysanthemum and cedar purling up from a little bronze frog on the floor near her bed reminded me of it all again. I stood gazing at the wide, quivering waterbed from which she'd been aroused. It was covered with a shroud of cloth-of-gold: millefleurs decorated its ground, ruby and sapphire-petalled, and the center was emblazoned with a great red stag that held suspended between its ninepoint rack a blazing emerald the size and shape of the heart. The rest of the studio was drab, the ancient factory walls painted the gray of cinderblock. The floor was all new hardwood, bleached and finished flat for dancing. And she in a gauze saffron robe with winged sleeves, its hem falling to her thick-sinewed dancer's ankles, revealing the knobs and callouses of her dancer's feet. Patting, pinching me, she circled round, laughing and restless, removing my clothing.

And the voice, hers as always, hoarse yet musical, though I never could hear its melody: she pitched her words strangely, so that the clear words she spoke were a language that said something else again. What, exactly, it was hard to know. Was that her powerful attraction? Perhaps. The face, with its heavy bones and wide green eyes, the heavy lips and large square teeth, was not beautiful, nor even handsome; the body was dense, strong, carrying its weight easily still at thirty-five. Not a comfortable body, and never graceful on the stage. She had failed at dancing, though it was her life. Dignity was all she owned. What is that today? A thing unknown. Yet I'd missed her truly when she was gone. Was it that barren pathos that attracted me? Perhaps. She was out of style, even her obsessive lust an anachronism in this world of frenzied, shallow greediness. Pointless, really. Too late: I was naked now.

And standing gazing at her bed. She dropped her robe. As she bent to strip that cover from the bed, I saw that her hips were blemished with yellowgreen bruises the size of fists, the flesh of her inner thighs traced over by a network of purple fine varicose, the ochre hair in her crotch a long, coarse shag tufting back between her buttocks. Even though the incense was drifting about her, the rank odor of her spread, dominating this space, slimesour, salt. With a moan deep in her chest, she threw herself down on the low bed, rolled over on her back and stared up at me from her great green sunken eyes as she opened herself wide— mouth, arms, legs. I fell upon her like an oak tree.

And we never slept. Later I rose to step behind the partition at the other end of the loft and void. My watch read 6:00. Outside, the streetlights burned in the hazy air before dawn; the trains were starting their morning run, clanking past hollowly below. The sweat of our struggle was crusting on my body in the stifling wintry morning. I was tired, but not eased in body or spirit. Something was terribly wrong. What had I found here?

And returning slowly from behind the partition, I see

something that stops me dead. She kneels in the middle of that wide, trembling bed, her arms crossed over her breasts, her head lolling, her deepset eyes half closed as if tranced. Two men squat on either side of her. I know them. One is her husband, that stolid broker of office buildings in midtown, a gray man with rough, gray skin. The other, his nephew, a lawyer and Mafia bagman, wiry, short, hooknosed and beetlebrowed. They lean against her. The older one presses close to her right side, his chin resting on her shoulder. The younger one presses one hand on her smooth knees, the other cupping his mouth as he whispers in her left ear in a low droning rapid mutter that sounds as though he is instructing her by means of a formula repeated over and over urgently. She sways forward and back, responding to the incantation with her entire being. They are taking possession of her, body and spirit. The words are indistinct: Nebrekkakka Membrekkakka, Membrekkakka Nebrekkakka. Seductive syllables.

And despite everything, despite my indifference, my freedom, my loathing of this whole evil time, I must save her. So intent are they on their filth, they never hear me as I sweep on them, naked as I am. Him I take by the throat in one surge, crushing the life's breath in him, lifting and flinging him aside like a wax figure. On the swing back, my joined fists catch that ferret between the eyes, knocking him cold. As his body tumbles to the floor, it seems to shrivel into a twitching ball of empty clothes.

And she remains kneeling, unmoved, unwakened, unknowing. Sunken into their power, sunken deep, deep. I slap her twice hard: a right, a left. Her head rolls on her shoulders, her body stays poised, upright, firmly balanced, the arms still crossed over her breasts. I am too late. She is lost to herself. The glassy eyes see nothing, the cheeks are inflamed, swelling, marked by my fingers, and blood trickles from her cut lip. The wreckage is appalling. Nothing is left in this place for me. The old man is as good as dead. His nephew will come to sooner or later, and put a contract out on my life. The year is ending purposelessly. I dress myself.

And as I left, I looked back once: in the weak light of the morning filtering through those dusty frosted panes I saw her kneeling still, as though at prayer. Naked, her dulled yellow hair strewn about her head in tangles like briars, the eyes closed now, her body swaying forward and back on that fluid bed. She seems made of some clayey rock. What kind of being is that?

And at last it is raining. The winter drought has ended, thank god. Sheets of grimy water run over the pavements, black currents coursing along the curbs, dragging paper and rags and bits of wood, the oily sludge flashing rainbows everywhere as the puddles back up from the clogged sewers. Things have not been thrown right. Things have fallen out this way instead.

GNOSIS

I WAS DRIVING through the midnight in my little white Fiat convertible. Thirsty, deathly tired, I'd pulled over and parked on the crumbling shoulder of the road, climbed out with some difficulty, and walked here up a steep hill through a ruined, black park. Now I stood looking back to get my bearings, and saw dimly that I'd parked on a kind of causeway running across a vast swampland whose watery tracts glistened beneath a night sky full of low, turbulent clouds lit up and glowing fitfully, bloodred, as though illumined not by sheet lightning but by silent, distant explosions, great fires burning in towns behind the hills around this valley. On the dismal plain through which this causeway ran, there were scattered leafless trees, gnarled, twisted, dead, and broken stumps, and fallen, rotting forest giants. I stood in the middle of a wooden bridge over what seemed a deep moat far below. I turned about again and looked at the high wall and the gate on this place: an age-slimed, rough-hewn stronghold. A fetid wind blew around it, breathing in damp gusts now hot, now cold. I realized I was not alone, that men and women were walking past me silently, going in and under the rusting portcullis, each one alone. They wore formal attire, dark coats, gray trousers, patent boots, and long dresses, velvet and satin jackets, jewels, and silk shawls. While I am buttoned in my white, belted raincoat, and wear twill trousers and a cashmere, turtleneck sweater, suede boots—driving clothes. Obviously I am only passing through, not dressed for the occasion.

In heavy silence they come up the hill on paths leading from the dark, swampy plain. They file by on both sides, as though heading to a State Wedding or State Funeral, or a Congress of Nations. I am tired, in need of some refreshment—it seems as though I have been driving forever. I shrug. I am here. I go on in too.

Having passed beneath the hanging portcullis, I find I am in the Great Court . And yes, someone is in charge here. A giant of a man, taller, bulkier, more powerful than I have ever seen—a Goliath. Bearded, widemouthed, square-toothed, someone out of the lost, epic days. As the men and women in their fancy dress file towards him, he receives each in turn, grasping hand and arm, embracing each one, his deep voice giving them low and hoarse directions it seems, for each one enters the castle by a low small door, each alone, and through many doors, like ratholes. I come to him and look up into his glaring, deepset, red eyes, round as saucers, as the Grimms would say. He waits for me to speak. His thick tongue lolls over his fat lips with amusement. I insist, I'm just passing through, you know. I don't belong here. I've got a very long way to go yet. Then he replies in a rumbling basso voice, "Welcome, my friend! My name is Cacooethes!" Graciously, he smiles in his stubbly beard, inviting me to join his organization. "Come in, my friend, this is my headquarters. My group is now in session. I would be pleased to have you become a member. You've arrived just in time."

Flattered by his deep, goodhumored and reassuring words, I am about to say yes. I hesitate, and as I pause, thinking about my choice, I seem to see him without his black jumpsuit. His body is hirsute, bear's tufts of thick, curly, blackbrown hair sprout from his shoulders, his chest is a morass of rusty boar bristles. Something about this makes me suspicious, perhaps the way people vanish through those little, low doors. His name puzzles me too. Perhaps I should turn and leave right away. Then it comes to me: this fellow is Satan's chief devil. Or, his name is a name for the Adversary himself! He seems to guess my apprehension. He smiles at me ingratiatingly, as if to excuse himself for not having shown himself directly to me—as if he could never be so rude. Soothingly, he says, "Don't worry, my friend, it's all right here." Opens his arms to embrace me. As our chests meet, I feel that I can discern his true form: he is not a flesh-and-blood giant. I see him as though suddenly gifted with vision: this doorkeeper is a boiler, an ironplated mechanical monster with eight arms, long steel rods with powerful steel grappling hooks for fingers! Inside this boiler is a sea of orangewhite flame. I hear his whispered roaring in my ears, "Caca, they call me." Oh yes, I say aloud, I know who you are!

It's too late! What is that roaring about my head, in my ears? A furnace. I am melting into him. He is absorbing me in the redwhite flames leaping inside that boiler of a body. And I too will become a devourer of souls. But this is an accident, I think, a misunderstanding! Because I was thirsty I left my car in the middle of my journey. Because I needed to relax, to stretch out a bit and rest. I had been driving alone so hard and so long. I only happened to stumble onto his operation—I hadn't come directly to his castle in his desolated district. I don't have to join his organization. I don't have to stay here. And I think, He's only just who he is. He just does what he does. And I can walk away before I'm utterly possessed by his flame... through which I am now able to see all those who had entered before me. They are no longer clothed in their formal attire, but naked now and joyous, cavorting about with limber glee, carrying on wildly, dancing and leaping in the fires like children in a swimming pool. Out there on the drawbridge, they passed me in silence, filing solemn from all directions of that cold, scorched moorland, while now here they are radiant with passion, with demonic intensity, released and transformed into souls shouting, singing amidst the flames.

Oh no, I think, I have to get back to the car before that gate crashes down! I break away from the clasp of that castiron boilerbody, and dash for the drawbridge and the outer darkness of the world—and my freedom there in the empty night.

PERCEVAL

So FAR, SO GOOD. The dossier shows progress from kindergarten on, all my doings sans hitch or blemish. But how's the selection made? A competition free to all comers, yet who are they? Your life an open book; theirs a mystery, sealed and silent. Until the story's finished, when what was hidden is revealed: their works and days: error and wastage, disguised as life. Meanwhile, you apply, and apply. You wait for the interview, which is the first real step, or perhaps the last. You must be ready, though there's no particular way to prepare.

When the letter came by SPECIAL DELIVERY early this morning, my eyes began to be opened, I thought. I was requested to show up at Seneca. So, that was the fortune behind the Fellowship! Gilded Age, Robber Baron money: railroads, shipping, coal and iron, and the banking that absorbed it all in our century. A massive segment of it now philanthropic, living its own life. For each lucky Fellow it offers freedom from care. Riches given to all through that singular award of freedom to an individual. Not quite first prize in the lottery, but it should suffice. A gift's a gift. Take it. Use it. Even if it's tainted by irregularity.

145

The small irregularity is, I suppose, this invitation to Seneca. Unless I'm too careful. Perhaps my journey there, which has taken five long years from my life, will lead to the interview? At the tiny dilapidated station an hour up the Hudson, I take a taxi. After a mile of driveway winding out beyond the high stone wall's automatic iron gates that opened and closed again with a quiet, well-oiled rumbling, there's the place. A low, fieldstone carriage house below had been shut up long ago: the lock on the door was rusted through and the windows dusty and darkened. There were fine views along this gravel road: copses of ancient oaks, tall stands of firs, plantations of grand sugar maples; small herds of deer browsing at the dark fringes of the woods in the distance, does and fawns; rabbits hopping over the green meadows that opened among the trees; and, on the thick lawn sloping up to surround the great granite sculpture—a Beaux Arts castle for a magnate—a flock of peahens with their cock in full display strutting before them and uttering harsh shrieks. As the cab pulls up, two black and white Great Danes bound alongside bellowing at us. They're friendly fellows, and I climb out unharmed— except that one of them rears to lick my face, leaving muddy pawprints the size of a child's hand on both shoulders of my jacket. A man steps forth and pulls him off, pummelling him and smiling, and directs me under the postern at the end of the open drawbridge that spans a dry moat full of blossoming purple and white lilac trees.

We have all seen a place like Seneca, in old movies or dreams, or read of it in childhood: the plutocrat's demesne: its empty suits of polished armor flanking the foyer, pikes, halberds and crossbows on the black oak-panelled walls, the massive antique English and Spanish furniture, the sumptuous Persian carpetings on the slate flagstone floor. Vast rooms to right and left. Cool on this June day: a hush that is palpable. It's still early afternoon, yet it's dark in here. In the sitting room on my right, sunlight plays through the leaded glass of the French windows, some of them opened to the rosegarden flashing its blobs of crimson and white, and beyond them the red clay of the tennis courts, and then the shimmering light green of the swimming pool, from which a groundsman is sweeping leaves and insects with a net on a long pole: the light sparkles in the water dripping from it. In the sky swallows swooping, twittering as they hunt.

I'm about to follow this footman—is that what he's called? he wears a blue linen dustcoat—upstairs, when the master of Seneca himself steps out of a door that should be the library there, off that sitting room—I glimpse books going up out of sight, a moveable oak ladder, a red leather Morris chair.... He's slipping tortoise-shelled reading glasses off with his right hand, fumbling them at the pocket of his blazer, a blue-green tartan with embossed golden buttons. He carries a thick sheaf of papers in a brown manila folder beneath his left arm. Baggy white flannel trousers; bare, varicosed feet in denim espadrilles. I hadn't imagined him bearded: scraggly, white fleece, his white hair shaggily cropped, a wen the size of a pearl onion above his left eyebrow. Rather scholarly looking, in fact. Why should I be surprised? What do I know? I am ignorant. He also seems surprised to see me, as though I am not only a stranger but unexpected too: he throws his head back to look up at me, squinting, and makes me feel loutish, towering over him here like this. His head waggles with the tremor of Parkinson's disease, yet he bears it with the authority of one who not only proposes, but disposes as well. Have I come at the wrong time? Surely there must be a regular traipse of guests over this wide threshold, what with the complexes of interlocking duties and business affairs to be managed, including the media conglomerate that is in effect his voice, worldwide.

As he approaches, hesitant, taking scuffling steps, as if he'd prefer to slip past me, I hold my hand out and announce my name. His eyebrows arch, vaguely quizzical. At his throat a blue polkadotted silk ascot is held in place by a cabuchon ruby, seventy-five bloody-coruscating carats at least. My name seems not to have enlightened him. Nonetheless he welcomes me instantly with his clasp: a broad palm, warm, dry, gentle. Though his fleshy pressure seems somehow impersonal too. In a low apologetic voice, he says, "I'm sorry. Wasn't expecting you. Perhaps my secretary's made a mistake." I feel myself flushing: I have made the mistake, and not my first. I, who've never arrived the right moment. Taking the letter from my breast pocket, I unfold it. No, this is the appointed day. "Well," he sighs, "it's all right then. You'll excuse me: I keep only a skeleton staff here now. And things are a bit rushed. It's one crisis or another. You won't mind being left on your own?" Well, sir, I begin, I'm sorry I'm a burden to you. "Not at all," he protests, kind yet absent too, holding onto my hand, "no one's a burden to me, my dear fellow, no one and nothing." He casts his eyes around this entrance hall, suggesting that there is room in this mansion for us all. "But I am in fact somewhat distracted these days. Too many plans. Never time to see them through." He has not let go my hand. He bites his upper lip: he's trying to think of something. "Tell me," he blurts, as if eagerly seeking my judgment, "while I have you here, what would you say to the establishment of this place as a reserve for a select group, so to speak... thinkers, and such? Is that idea obsolete?" Well, sir, I've just walked in here, and— "Ah, it's a waste, you mean. Much too late to devote ourselves to that quest. I thought so." I venture to contradict him: Isn't that why I was asked here? "Oh, you do thinking then? Really?" Again, I feel my face flame with the fire of embarrassment—do I? "Never mind, we'll come to it later. Just now there's no time, is there. You'll think I'm indifferent to your fate. I am not. Believe me."

To this politeness, I nod gratefully. He releases my hand at last and turns aside, saying we're to meet at supper, I must make myself at home here if I can, and disappears through another heavy, oak door on the left. The footman escorts me to my suite upstairs, tosses the overnight case on a stand, throws the narrow casements wide, and leaves. The scene offers a wonderful sweep of lawns, woods and land rolling up to a ridge on which a hill bursts steeply out of the treetops, bare, glowing umber in the afternoon light, a crenellated tower on its crown, its windows flaring. That is the only structure visible, about five miles off: everything out there is Seneca, stretching to the high horizon.

By the window, there's an elegant kneehole desk of inlaid wood and mother-of-pearl: the top shows a stag at bay, one hound tearing at his throat, others fastening fangs into his flank. A Waterford carafe and tumblers stand on it. I pour one full of whiskey and wash three aspirin down. The profound quiet here, after the clattering, filthy commuter cars, empty on the midday run up the shore of the Hudson, has unmasked a throbbing headache I was not aware of till now. It will take a while getting used to the spaciousness here, the atmosphere drenched with moist light that fills up this basin among the old hills...after ten years' confinement in the roachraddled rooms I call my home on Avenue A at 13th Street, just off St. Mark's Place. While I wait for the aching band to dematerialize in my head, I dab a soapy towel at the black pawprints the beast left on my jacket. Unsuccessfully. I give it up—no point in wetting it through and having to wear it damp all evening. I have nothing else with me but a pair of shorts, a new poloshirt, sneakers and swimtrunks. I own nothing but this old seersucker suit, the worn, white suede bucks and the frayed tie. A wanderer hardly needs that much, in fact.

I could read. Or write: a quire of handmade paper and a good pen are laid out on the desk, on which there's also a silver budvase, with a perfect redyellow rose, freshly cut: a dewdrop sparkles in its heart. Was I expected after all? I can't focus my eyes for reading, and I have nothing to write. After ten minutes, I've finished the rich, malt scotch, and the utter tranquility of the room, the slow drift of small, white cumulus clouds past the tower out there begins to be oppressive: the jangle of my nerves, my own pulse in my head and my breathing are too audible in this peace. I must move about.

The hallway's empty. My wing of this castle seems devoid of life: the other eleven bedroom suites are vacant, as I find on opening the doors on rooms like mine, each with its lovely rose in its slender vase. No luggage anywhere. I am the only guest then, truly unexpected though my invitation was correctly written? I'll have to accept it, since I am here.

Over the lobby, a wide, curved balcony. Paintings adorn it, some good, some great, in fact, the sort you might see in books, not in the museum. I pace down the grand stairs, following the pictures hung along it. At the turning, there's a Renoir nude that must be seen to be believed, so full of light is it, brilliance that even in this darkening afternoon seems to well up from the depths of its surface. She, rather it, is incredibly effulgent, the smile she wears . . . my coming here's already amply rewarded by this sight of her, even if it's error in the end, pointless waste. I can go back where I came from, sustained: this vision is enough.

Once down, I continue pursuing the wall of art back along the hall beneath the staircase. And then I hear remote voices, from somewhere below. A door's ajar, hidden in the gloom under the balcony. A stairway, narrow, steep. The voices are hollow, not in conversation: remarks, or commands, punctuated by feet dragging and stopping. Thuds, clinking. I decide to sneak down and see.

The stone steps stop in a large pantry, cool and filled with the purring of a bank of freezers and refrigerators. This pantry gives onto a great, low, vaulted kitchen furnished with hanging racks of pots and pans, and longhandled culinary tools, tables, benches, ovens and paired heavyduty ranges and stainless steel sinks. It's not a basement, however. The land must drop away on this side of the building, because the honeyed late afternoon light pours through its glass wall, filling the whole place with cheery radiance. A chef with his tall white hat, his cheeks glistening pink above a pouting mouth, his apron tight over a nice round belly, is trussing a goose. Beside him on his maple worktable lies a shiny pink haunch of veal, a fifty-pound loin at least. Beside it three bluewhite capons, necks and heads still feathered and dangling bleeding on the immaculate black and white tesselations of the tiled floor, waiting their turn to be dressed. The chef's assistant—a lanky and sallow fellow with long, thin moustaches, apron hitched round just under his armpits, white tee-shirt torn at the neck, his long sinewy arms tattooed with flowers, anchors, hearts and bannered mottoes, and, yes, a fat Cupid with drawn bow over the right triceps—notices me standing in the door. A cigarette droops from one side of his mouth: his eye winks against its purling smoke. He faces the chef at an adjacent worktable, and goes on swiftly chopping big red onions. Near them is a wire basket of peeled potatoes, bunches of thick carrots, a colander of sweetpeas, bowls of wax beans and heaps of tomatoes, cucumbers, celery and lettuces and red radishes. The man who'd carried my bag sits at a low table, polishing flatware: a coffee service waits to be rubbed bright too. At one of the sinks, there's a chubby, blond potboy, violently pimpled and crewcut, swabbing out a copper cauldron, sweating and grumbling to himself. These were the voices I had heard as they hummed, joked, responded to the chef's curt demands. This, the skeleton staff? Serving an empty house? For whom is this feast being prepared? Who will break the sweet loaves yeasting on the range? taste the cherry tarts glowing in those little aluminum pans? Who will drink these three jeroboams of Chateau Petrus '59 standing uncorked to breathe out of the way here in the pantry?

I have been enjoying their orderly activity, and am about to cross the kitchen to look into the huge stockpot steaming on the other range—its sharp scent of herbs and fatty marrow wafts across this breezy chamber—when I notice a long table next to the wall just to my left, and remain fixed where I am. On this marble slab, halfcovered by a rag of stained sheeting, a body, the nude body of a young woman. The sheet's carelessly, even hastily draped over her. She lies crumpled there on her right side, arms and legs askew, bent brokenly at elbows and knees, as though she's fallen from a great height. Her flesh is pale cream, bruised with splotches large as my hands. Her head's tilted up at a cruel angle. I drift sideways towards her, tempted to lift the sheet from the face it masks. I'm afraid to. Yet I cannot prevent myself from touching the part of her upper arm showing from beneath the cover, or pressing that portion of her thigh protruding over the edge of the slab. Her naked flesh is firm, not yet cold.

Inside my skull I hear my own voice whisper— She's been killed. But in fact my lips are sealed. I'm here in their midst, after all. And they know she is here too. They know where I stand, what I've seen. One of them must have tossed this poor covering over the beautiful cadaver, the bit of drapery a Bathing Artemis clutches to her in one dimpled hand as she steps unprotected and shy from the secret pool...to conceal her modesty from me, the unexpected guest. The chef's carving away at the haunch of veal. The chef's helper chops loudly at carrots with his great blade. They all go right on with their tasks. These people make their own rules, I murmur soundlessly.

My fingers tingle with the sensation of her flesh; my ears are flooded with the silence of her smashed form. Taking a deep breath, I go on ahead into the kitchen to inspect the makings of the banquet. They can appreciate my *sangfroid*. I have seen what I should not: I know what I must not know. A missing girl. I, who was not seeking her, have found her. The damage is done. I must not betray myself. Still, silence is testimony too.

I walk confidently through them to gaze down into the swirling broth of the stockpot, to sniff up its fragrant vapor—pepper and salt, parsley, marjoram, cumin and thyme—and to contemplate the big bones knocking and bumping at its bottom. I shall dine well here.

MAYA

I HAD GONE DOWN to central America with a scientific expedition to explore a site high in the mountains. We'd been scouting around in the jungle for a month and discovered nothing at all. After the first week I found myself becoming rather sceptical, detached from their intense search: they were checking everything: the flora, fauna, insects, geology, meteorology. No clues.

We had with us there a local Indian, a hermit so old his skin was like gray clay, wrinkled and folded with aged emaciation: his bent skeleton and stringy, taut sinews and veins seemed to be all he was made of. We thought of him as the last surviving member of whatever people had once been there, if any had. And indeed he seemed to me of high caste, a chief or priest, a head Inca or whatever. He had appeared out of the forest to guide us: he cooked for us and gave puzzling directions, which however never came to anything. A typical native informant.

On the last day of our sojourn, my colleagues decided to make a final desperate effort to find something to be able to write up in the report to the foundation in New York that had given us substantial grant money. They could be heard down there in the thick jungle crashing about, calling to each other, hacking and chopping away, now here, now there, like beaters on a big game hunt. I had given up and remained behind in camp. I walked up and sat on the naked hilltop above our tents to enjoy the sun and watch the formations of white cumulus clouds scudding overhead. The air was fresh and cool up here. I thought how odd this is: there was our camp, pitched below the hilltop that was crowned by a flat space surrounded by low stone walls, a ruin with broken columns of what surely must have been a temple once upon a time, or so it seemed to me—and yet not one clue had they found, nothing that could inform us of the lost people we had come to seek. Perhaps all that was left of their language and history was this old man now shuffling up the hillside towards me.

He stands before me at last, all bent and gnarled, and asks what we have found. I tell him that we'd scratched and dug everywhere in this place, and our hands remain empty. He smiles gently, knowingly, as I expound upon what we thought, or rather what *they* thought they were hunting for: a lost civilization. "Come," he says, "and sit down here with me." And he leads me to one corner of this ruined space, where there is a massive round stone table about six inches thick, roughhewn and mossy with age. Stone benches are planted about it, their feet welded deep in the thick, naked clay.

We sit at the table awhile in silence. I am listening to the birds chatter and call everywhere, flitting in and out of the fringe of the jungle below us. I can still hear the frenzied crashing of the scientists in its depths, like a herd of swine. Then the old man smiled, and I smiled back at him. His head was tied round with a filthy old red clout and he wore tattered homespun breeches. Then he said, "I have decided to give you what you want." He stood up again, leaned over his seat and lifted it as if he were opening the lid of a piano bench. Although that slab of basalt was four inches thick, it tilted up easily. Inside, there were rolls of white sheets. Clear, thin, fine vellum tubes. They were ancient yet perfectly preserved. I glimpsed diagrams, patterns of lines, drawings and whole dense paragraphs of text—strange hieroglyphs. "Here," he says, "is the record of the history of our nation, an empire gone forever. I think you will have the means of reading our lost language, and you will understand the source of our powers. There are forms that still remain for you to find. I give it all to you!"

I felt doubt dwelling in me. And I felt that I must not take them. But also, I said—So, they do exist after all! And all this time they have been lying right here where we are sitting! But you must know, old man, I am not sure you should reveal them to my friends, or give me the responsibility of possessing them. I think the power in them too great: it will not be used wisely. Frankly, I don't trust their understanding. I think that they will abuse such information. Perhaps this knowledge ought to remain secret.

He smiled, knowing that now he'd shown me it was utterly impossible to hide this matter again. Such is the nature of revelation. "You must take them," he says quietly. "Here."

I was shivering with excitement—a vast treasure of history. Yet I was also aware that I was frightened by the knowledge I knew would be exposed to me when, back home again in New York, I had at last deciphered the scrolls. How would I be able to keep the secret of such power from the world? How could I make it safe for the future? Who could protect me now?

VALLEY

IT IS AXIOMATIC, my old teacher maintained, that to do good work demands submersion in, and identification with, your subject. My silence in seminars signified resistance to his lesson. He warned me that, although I might go on to make a name for myself, sometime, somewhere, I must find myself faced with the choice: either enter the human situation, or abandon all hope of understanding.

What if I refuse? In that case I should be finished, he said, and my life would have been wasted. I raised my eyebrows. "You think me a coward for not refusing." I sighed and said nothing. He tilted back in the old oak chair behind the heavygrained, dark and scarred oak desk he'd brought to his new office. These relics of the last century, the legacy of his teacher, didn't go at all with the new bronze, anodized aluminum bookcases and functional office furniture the University had installed in this air-conditioned, glass and stainless-steel showcase for social science, flush with grants of millions from the Institutes of Mental Health and the National Science Foundation. "And you even think I'm a fool. Why? Because I've accepted the human lot? Let me tell you this: it's the only way to learn anything worth knowing." He stuffs that rough shag into his sour, burned-out briar, and lights it with blackened, horny fingers, their long nails yellowed and caked with filthy dottle. Still I say nothing. Which upsets him. Which seems a continued denial. He adds, absolutely, and puffing away, "And, the only way to live. You'll find out. Whether you like it or not."

And it is twenty years later that I have recalled that late spring day in his office just before noon. I can see, as if I were still sitting facing him, the sweet, fresh green leaves of the ancient elm trees on the wide lawn surrounding that building. New leaves of milky, light green that made the great canopies glow with the dewy and moving light that poured into them from the Midwestern June sky. Tall elms, with thick yet graceful, grayblack trunks, finely-ridged, that soared up and outward like the slender forms of caryatids, silent women with arms that extended out in long, drooping branches, immense women hidden in the delicate youthfulness of that species of tree. I'd forgotten that hour for twenty years. It comes to me now in this darkness, in this waiting solitude in which I sit, seventy feet below the surface of the earth, at the bottom of a smooth, round shaft, in the Valley of Sacrificing.

He'd taught us well, actually. Our group, his choice students, coming to him at the end of the epoch of discoveries, had succeeded everywhere. Meticulous observers, prodigious collectors, respected recorders and analysts of the peoples we had joined. Our books were many, and became immediately contemporary classics. We'd done splendidly for science, and for humanity. What it had cost us, even we did not know. How could we? What is there but success?

And yet all along, in many difficult conditions, I knew

that the choice that he'd said waited for me somewhere, sometime, had not presented itself. Where was it, then? And when it appeared, blocking my way, must I believe that I should have to give up human understanding? Was there truly no other way to live?

My stool is a rough block of granite. The vertical shaft overhead is about six feet in diameter: there is no means by which one could hope to ascend it. The daylight up there, visible as a pale, shimmering blue-white disk no larger than a silver dollar, is brightening. Soon the sun will pass over and send a dazzling beam straight down to illuminate my spherical chamber.

I know quite well, after years of visiting these people, what this situation is. And I know as well as they do what it means. Once a year, for the wellbeing of the nation, when the sun shall come to pass directly over the mouth of a shaft sunken into the earth, there will be a sacrifice. This nation is not cruel or wanton. Neither is it stupid, insensitive, or savage. The people will soon enough be indistinguishable from the rest of humanity, getting, spending, producing and consuming more or less efficiently. In such a matter as this, however, some things remain the same, and time has no significance. The Valley of Sacrificing is a wide plain beside a round, shallow lake. It is surrounded by the high walls of a long extinct volcanic crater, mountain-high walls, fertile, and planted with orchards and gardens, all terraced by concentric rings that run right to the top. Their thirteen villages lie at the foot of the slope, in a circle of twenty-eight miles. In the center of the cone are the lake and this plain, which is dotted with many thousands of these shafts, each covered with a carved stone, like a manhole cover, or sun disk. The whole mosaic constitutes a useful calendar of great antiquity and unperturbed accuracy, although there may be shafts that have been used more than once in the long millenia. The people, however, insist not. They claim this as the one constant, the only truth in the world they know. Great sceptics, my people. But I am a greater sceptic yet. Perhaps my eyebrows lifted and revealed my thought. Perhaps that is why I woke to find myself here at the bottom of this shaft.

I never suspected that they would punish me in this manner. I am not suitable either, I had thought, as victim or hero. Or hero-victim. In their own way they are gentle, even civilized. If fixed in this ritual. They must have placed me down here as I slept; for that, they must have put me into a deep, long slumber.

I have been down a dozen of these shafts. At the bottom of each there lies a skeleton. There are the usual utensils for sustaining life, or comforting it afterwards: a dish, a flask, a cup. Nothing more: no jewelry, no tools, no weapons. Except for a wellmade knife of flint, or a sharp obsidian blade, or horned antler. The meaning of that instrument is obvious: the victim had been given food, but he was also expected to become a hero—to offer himself to the sun at the hour in which its blinding glare stands overhead filling the hole on the one day of the year. How many of these bones, though, had been heroic?

For some years I'd wondered what the sacrifice underwent, what it meant for him? One knows what it is worth to the nation, to the way people are situated in the world, to the structure of organized social life: by this one constant they have persisted from the beginning. Yet who has discovered what it is for the victim? Without that knowledge, what is all the rest worth? You have been sent ahead, sent out, offered up to the goal of our human existence—and what you achieve remains absolutely unknown to those for whom you had gone. So here now is my opportunity to learn what all should know. It is in fact a gift, a great gift. I am not surprised to receive it, after all.

But where is my dish, my flask, my cup? Where the knife for my food, and for my self-immolation? I am naked and cold and hungry instead. But, knowing my people, I am patient too. They will do this right, as in everything else, or so it has seemed to me over the years of my study.

And it is good to think also that while I am given my chance to know what I have always wished and thought essential to know, I shall also be conferring the usual, expected benefits upon the people. Nothing better can be imagined.

At last, sounds from above. I look up. The round opening is darkened: something blocks the light. It moves. I watch, trying to grasp what I see. Finally, as the occluding form seems to be turning and dwindling, I realize that someone is being lowered down the shaft. As he descends, he seems to shrink, because his approaching body doesn't fill the entire cylinder. A trick of perspective? But also apprehended truly, for finally, seated in a loop of thick rope, is a boy of no more than twelve. Naked, beardless, beautiful, innocent of any understanding. He has been washed, curled, polished with oil. On his lap, the dish, with a loaf of bread, the flask, containing whatever fermented drink is thought suitable—I can scent its vinous fumes already—and the cup, all of rough, undecorated, unglazed clay. Also, a fine, long blade of steel. My own knife, in fact. They have displayed their subtle thought and gentle courtesy. They have honored me.

Seated, dandled in the swaying rope, the boy recites a formula, singsong as children do with words they have memorized. These are secret words. Ancient words. They can have no meaning for the child, of course. To the one who hears, they are everything. And I listen carefully. I must not forget them. I must remember them. I must take them with me.

He finishes. He hands me the dish, the flask, the cup.

With the knife he hesitates. It lies across his smooth thighs as he sits in the loop, turning easily, swinging like a pendulum.

Tell me again, I say. He smiles, and repeats his strange recitation. I have it now. I do not know what the words signify, but I have them by heart now. What more is needed?

I take the knife. The child smiles. I have never seen this lad in my village. He must be a changeling. Human sacrifice has been outlawed for many years by the great world, but some remote nations still practice it in this way: they exchange children between villages. It is not proven; but one intuitively knows it.

With one swift thrust, I have severed his neck from ear to ear. It is a terrible sight, but the sun at that moment overhead fills the shaft with light, and I am so dazed that I am spared the sight of the child's ruined body, which with one swift motion I have thrown from the swinging cable's loop, and replaced with myself.

I am winched up, slowly, slowly, to the surface of the world again. When I step forth among my people, my hand and arm coated with blood like the crusted knife, they step back, withdrawing from me in a widening ring, appalled at what I've done. In silence, they turn away. I know that I shall never be able to speak with them again. I have made the great refusal. I have left all community behind me for good, forever. I do have the old words, words that came from the remote past, words that lead to a future unimaginable. But nothing else. And to whom should I ever utter them? Yet what it was most important to know, the knowledge that may be gained only by having remained below to die, I shall never have the chance to learn again.

THE BIRD CAGE

THE STORM must have swept in some time before dawn. When I woke, I lay listening in the darkness to that metallic December rain lowering over the city, pouring in cold gusts of shrapnel against the windows. The light turned gray, but never much more than gray all morning; the rain fell full of razors against the walls, as if it meant to scour this century's bitter grime from brick and stone, and wash away the sludge coating the town like an impenetrable callous of lacquer laid on year by year and fixing everything we are in a sterile waste.

I didn't go to work. Towards noon I put on my rubbers, wrapped myself in my wool-lined raincoat, unfurled my umbrella and went to keep a lunch appointment at the Four Seasons with an old friend who is a professor of political science. Alex is an urbane, sceptical man, and his third book on naval warfare has just been named a Pulitzer Prize volume. It is also a Book-of-the-Month Club selection, and already a Bancroft History Award winner, which has helped it sell over a half-million copies. Alex is suddenly rich. Today is his sixty-fifth birthday and he is beginning his celebration with me alone, in honor, he remarks, of my silence.

I toast his inevitable, late success, and we order oysters and a brace of squabs stuffed with wild rice and accompanied by braised morels and a '61 Margaux, baked pears for dessert and espresso. He tells me now that he has never been to sea, and the only battleship he's ever seen was parked at the Brooklyn Naval Yard. His career began with a dissertation in Classics, an analysis of the confusion at the Battle of Actium. His mother had read *Antony and Cleopatra* to him when he was nine years old and semi-delirious with rheumatic fever. His damaged heart put him at a desk in naval intelligence during the war, where he fiddled with battle reports far from any action, and wrote up commendations for commanders' medals. His colleagues have always resented his top clearance, the reviewers call him a crypto-militarist. His work, he avers, is simply dispassionate analysis of webs of lies woven about the accidental maneuvers of masses of men at the mercy of wind and wave: neither art nor science nor traditions rule the warring fleets, though he has never said so before. His laurels surprise him: it means merely that no one knows anything about anything. "What can we extrapolate from ignorance. Now, Caesar understood the language of the birds, and he taught it to Mark Antony. But Antony was rash: he insulted the Pythia at Delphi. The hag silenced the birds from that time on. Not even sparrows would chatter in his presence after that. He was doomed."

Alex took a cab over to the Century Club: he wanted to smoke his cigar and browse through the Audubon quietly until cocktails, when he will be honored by a reception and banquet laid on by his publisher. I went out and walked up to the Park through that freezing rain. Outside the Plaza, one old closed hansom stood forlorn, its lantern glowing weakly, the nag covered with a poncho, his head drooping to his knees. A halfdozen ragged sparrows cowered in the poor shelter of his belly, waiting for some grain to spill when he tosses his muzzle to get at the mash sogging in the bottom of his nose bag.

There was no one but the animals at the Zoo. Under that pelting black sky towards four p.m. the gray light was already fading into an evening that would never come. The air wallowed with blasts of icy wind circling from the east and hurling the rain in sheets. I turned into a doorway and waited. The downpour grew heavier yet. I went inside. It was the aviary, warm and steamy. The place had been changed since I'd last been there. Now it was all one great cage with narrow winding paths among tiny pools and artificial rivulets under a thin forest of bare trunks and low palm trees and bushes. The collection seemed to be general, composed of waders, raptors, mountain and forest birds, tropical and temperate alike: parrots, macaws, toucans, small ducks, curlews, cranes, herons, flamingoes, doves and ducks, guinea fowl, hawks, ravens, crows, vultures and eagles. The small birds paddled about and splashed, the waders stalked sleepily, and the greater birds of prey skulked on their naked branches. One great horned owl hooted now and then, frightening none of the others: food was abundant here, and the birds paid no regard to the people who walked about among them with cameras on bright days. I was alone here, though. I sat on a little cast-concrete bench beside a six-inch waterfall, and watched the peacock preen himself, his tail spread out over a patch of dull brown sand. The rain poured steadily on the glass panes of the roof. I looked at the bank of thermostats and hygrometers attached to the trunk of a palm tree and thought, I have not had a thought in years.

Footsteps on the gravel. A tall woman approaching. She moves very slowly, and stops every other pace to gaze down at the waterfowl standing on one locked long leg, their heads tucked beneath a wing or beady eyes fixed on nothing. A long, gray, leather coat wraps her; it is buttoned and belted, despite the lush warmth in the bird cage. Her hair is thick, white, brushed back from her high forehead; it is that stained white of women whose hair was flaxen in youth. Her face is masked to the cheeks by the fur collar of her coat, a yellowish muff it is now, soiled by the filthy rain of this city, and tatty with age too. She does not pass by me, but rather stops to stand facing me at arms' length. She is very tall: my head, where I sit, comes only to the height of her thighs. Looking up towards her uptilted face, I see only the large nostrils of a fine aquiline nose: she is staring at the great owl high behind me. I turn to see what he's doing. Nothing: he perches on that bare, artificial limb of the dead tree trunk, a big, motheaten clump, his enormous yellow eyes full of shattered crystal, wide open, hexagonal unblinking orbs steady under her gaze.

I break my silence— I come here to look at the birds. I come to hear them. "I know you do," she says. "But I come to see the birds. I come here to listen to them." I've come ever since childhood, I add. The place has changed, hasn't it. "I've always come. But it's the same." No, we can be closer to the birds now. "Closer, but not any nearer." Oh? I say.

She looks down at me, smiling to herself, as if amused by my remarks. Her face is round and full, with high cheekbones. I stand up, and find she is a good full head taller than I. She wears no makeup: her yellowish complexion shows a velvety skin, not furred but covered with a network of minute fine lines. She was, once upon a time, not unhandsome. Wide, gray eyes, flecked with faint ochre. As she stands there she seems to sway very slowly from the waist, the way a tall pine sways in the air on a mountainside. The scent that comes from her is resinous too, heavier and softer than that chemical pinetree essence some soaps exude.

How did you know I come here? I ask. "I am a poet," she replies, still gazing at the owl over my shoulder, "and I know things like that. I've come here since the beginnings. I saw the first and I saw the second levels of these walls built on." She describes the hidden foundations here, as though this dingy, granite-bricked building in Central Park were erected upon the lower courses of handfitted cyclopean blocks, and those blocks themselves hewn from the knees of Mount Parnassus and laid down like the floor of the temple sanctuary. Kidding her along, I ask, So, you can remember what's buried under our feet here? "If poetry must be made, it can be made from stones," she answers simply, "even out of stones, since bare stones are all we have." I wouldn't know, I say. "We veil ourselves in our own darkness," she adds, speaking to the owl with that low, oracular and indifferent voice. I wouldn't know, I say again, stubbornly.

The peacock screams twice, and, folding his great fan of purple eyes into a long train, paces carefully away from us. For the first time, she looks at me, her eyes filming over. Her lips curl with contempt. They are full lips and dark red. She turns from me, whispering, "No, you wouldn't know, would you."

I watch her move away slowly, and now I perceive that she is really an old woman: her torso is propped upon legs as thick, and as shapeless as columns of stone, swollen from ankle to hip. She swings first one, then the other forward heavily, her long body rocking from side to side as she progresses, scraping the gravel with her toes. Down her back, her hair flows like a bleached, coarse mane.

Suddenly the alarm bell sounds, warning everyone that it's time to leave. Closing time. The prolonged clanging disturbs the mixed population of birds, and they leap fluttering from the ground, splashing up distracted from the shallow wading pools. The smaller birds swirl round the great cage with a flittering of wings, the larger ones flap and float about in random circles and criss-crossings, cawing, crying, clattering their beaks in a terrible discordance. The owl lifts his wings and beats them emptily, shifting his grip on the perch from foot to foot.

I button up and step outside into the dark, December downpour. There is no one and nothing in sight.

THE OLD MUSE

MIDNIGHT. I have returned to the Bronx. Allerton Avenue as it was nearly forty years ago. And I am forty years older, standing waiting outside that mausoleum, the Manufacturers Trust Company. No one is about under the yellowed street light. Overhead, the empty El station. Across the avenue, a lone Checker cab parked at the taxi stand. An old woman comes out of the darkness toward me. She is gaunt. She wears a loose cotton gown, a muu-muu printed with large dark flowers, blurred purple bruises. Her gray hair is wild, splaying over her shoulders in greasy hanks. Her eyes are hollowed with grief, her face creased with sleeplessness. She raises both skinny arms like an ancient votary approaching an altar, and comes directly to me, her eyes fixed upon my breast as though she looked through me, as though I were not there at all, and she drops those stiff hands on my shoulders, dead weights with clamping fingers. Her right arm slips downward slowly, tracing its clawfingers on my skin, over my heart. Yet I am not frightened: I stand still, frozen, patient. The magnetic force of her gesture is a silent thought, a command: *I must speak the truth. I must speak it out.* I am startled, but resigned to it too. I think, Why me? And I also think, So be it.

169

ABOUT THE AUTHOR

Born in New York City on Thanksgiving Day of 1929, Jascha Kessler has received many awards and fellowships for his fiction, poetry, plays, and translations, including two Senior Fulbright Awards. In 1979 he became the first American writer to be honored with the Hungarian PEN Club's Memorial Medal for his translations of Geza Csáth and Miklós Radnóti. Since 1961 he has been a Professor of English and Modern Literature at U.C.L.A. Mr. Kessler has lectured throughout Europe and South America, serves as American editor for *Art & Poetry Today* (New Delhi), and produces a regular book review program for radio stations KUSC-FM and KCPB-FM.